The La[st] Wunambi's Warning

Marvina Mind
Copyright © 2025 Marvina Mind

All rights reserved.

DEDICATION

To Sherlock, my ever-faithful companion, who walked beside me through sunlit days and stormy nights. Your wagging tail, boundless curiosity, and gentle soul brought joy beyond words.

Though you now roam beyond the park paths, your spirit lingers in every rustling leaf, in every playful breeze, in every quiet moment of remembrance.

You were more than a beagle—you were family. This is for you.

DISCLAIMER

This is a work of fiction. Names, characters, places, events, and incidents are either the product of the author's imagination or used fictitiously.
Any resemblance to actual persons, living or dead, actual events, or real locations is purely coincidental.

The views and opinions expressed by characters do not reflect those of the author, and any interpretations are left to the reader's discretion.

CONTENTS

	Acknowledgments	i
1	The Roaring Goldfields	1
2	Whispers at The Waterhole	6
3	Wunambi	11
4	The End of An Era	26
5	Modern Day	28
6	The Outcrop	33
7	The Legend of Jim Sullivan	36
8	The First Death	38
9	Back in Town	43
10	Return to the Kookaburra	50
11	The Watchers	54
12	The Cave of Secrets	60
13	What Next?	64
14	MinTech	68
15	Meeting of Minds	72
16	The Land Remembers	76
17	The Wunambi's Warnings	81
	Epilogue	89

ACKNOWLEDGMENTS

I acknowledge the Traditional Custodians of the land on which this story was written and shared, the Whadjuk Noongar people. I pay my deepest respects to their Elders, past and present, and to all First Nations people who continue to care for this Country.

This land has always been, and always will be, Noongar Boodja. It holds the stories, traditions, and knowledge of the Noongar people, whose connection to this land stretches back tens of thousands of years.

I recognise the strength, resilience, and wisdom of First Nations communities, and I acknowledge the ongoing impact of colonisation.

The inclusion of Wongi (Wangkatha) culture, including the mythic Wunambi, is a respectful fictional interpretation of Aboriginal spirituality. I acknowledge the Wongi people, traditional custodians of the Kalgoorlie region, and pay my respects to Elders past and present. Elements of Dreamtime lore have been drawn from general public knowledge, with the intent to honour, not appropriate. Any errors are my own.

Sometimes, life pushes us in unexpected directions. Through challenges and hardships, we find the strength to carve our own path. This book marks the beginning of a new adventure—one born from resilience, self-discovery, and the pursuit of something greater. To those who taught me what love is—and what it is not—thank you for leading me here.

CHAPTER 1
THE ROARING GOLDFIELDS

Kalgoorlie, Western Australia – 1896. A red sun hung low in the afternoon sky, casting long shadows over the dusty plain. Dozens of canvas tents flapped in a hot breeze on the outskirts of Kalgoorlie's bustling tent city. Ever since rich gold had been discovered a few years before, this once-desolate "Karlkurla" (as the local Wongi people called the place) swarmed with life. In less than a decade, the colony's population had quadrupled, drawing fortune-seekers from across Australia and the world. Most were young men chasing the glitter of gold, with only their hard luck and harder hope as companions. Now, those prospectors trudged through streets of packed earth, their boots kicking up clouds of fine red dust under a vast, unforgiving sky.

Jim Carter squinted against the glare as he guided his weary horse along Hannan Street – little more than a wide track lined with tents and makeshift timber shanties. His shirt was stained with sweat and ochre dust. At his side rode Patrick "Paddy" O'Rourke, an Irish digger whose spirits were far brighter than the threadbare clothes he wore. They had travelled together from Coolgardie after rumours of new alluvial gold find near a remote waterhole east of town. Both men's faces were etched with the grit and determination born of long days under the blazing sun and cold starry nights on the open plain.

Around them, Kalgoorlie boomed with chaotic energy. Hannan Street bustled with horse-drawn wagons delivering supplies, and prospectors haggling for tools and water. Women in plain cotton dresses carried baskets of provisions or hurried between canvas residences. A camel train led by Afghan cameleers padded by silently, strange and regal, loaded with bulging water barrels. The smell of woodsmoke, unwashed bodies, and frying bush scones mingled in the dry air. Amid the clamour, the Exchange Hotel – one of the few sturdier buildings in town – offered weary miners a warm beer and a brief escape. Jim and Paddy had little money for such luxuries; instead, they aimed to resupply and head straight out to stake a claim before others caught wind of the rumour.

As they passed a cluster of Wongi people camped at the town's edge, Jim tugged his horse to a slower pace. A group of Aboriginal children stared with wide dark eyes at the endless procession of wadjela (foreigners) streaming through their homeland. An elderly Wongi man stood by, wrapped in a threadbare blanket despite the heat, watching the newcomers with a mix of curiosity and wariness. Jim met the elder's gaze and offered a polite nod. The old man raised a hand in acknowledgment but did not smile. Jim felt a pang of unease – or perhaps guilt. He knew this land had belonged to the Wongi long before men like him tore into it seeking gold.

"You alright, Jim?" Paddy asked, noticing his friend's distraction.

Jim cleared his throat. "Aye. Just thinking...how strange it must be for them, seeing their land overrun like this."

Paddy glanced back at the camp. "Strange times, mate. Gold changes everything, like it or not."

Jim nodded silently. He recalled stories of how earlier gold strikes at Coolgardie had brought not only fortune but also disease and disorder. Typhoid fever had swept through the goldfields like a bushfire, cutting down men in their prime. Water was as precious as gold out here – without the planned water pipeline from Perth, life teetered on the edge. In town, condensers constantly boiled brackish groundwater, trying to make it drinkable. Men would pay a shilling a gallon for fresh water, and many more perished from thirst and sickness. The Aboriginal people, he knew, had always known where to find water – the hidden soaks and gnamma holes in the granite – but now many of those were being fouled or claimed by settlers.

They reached the assay tent where a government mining warden was recording claims. A queue of prospectors waited, dusty and impatient. The two friends hitched their horses and joined the line to register their intent for a new claim out east. Paddy hummed an Irish lullaby under his breath as they waited, fiddling with a small lucky medallion of St. Patrick around his neck. Jim scanned the crowd. Sunburnt faces, beards bleached by sun and dust, eyes alight with either hope or desperation – sometimes both. Each man carried the weight of dreams or nightmares in equal measure.

Near the front of the line, a tall man with a handlebar moustache argued with the warden. "What d'ye mean, I can't peg that ground? It ain't taken!" he barked.

"It's a reserve, Mr. Sloane," the warden replied coolly. "No prospecting allowed within a hundred yards of the native waterhole at Halfmoon. Government orders."

The man's face flushed red with anger. "Native reserve? Even the locals don't even use it! It's a damned waste – there's gold on that patch, I know it!" He slammed a fist on the rickety table.

Jim recognised the man – Charles Sloane, owner of a local supply store and rumoured to support many prospectors with equipment for a cut of their finds. Sloane was known to be greedy and influential. If he was interested in that area, Jim's hunch about its potential value grew stronger.

The warden held firm. "The law's clear. That area around Halfmoon Waterhole is off-limits for mining. Too many complaints were made that it's sacred to the Wongi. If you've got an issue, take it up with the Mining Board in Perth."

Sloane glared but bit back any further argument. He noticed Jim and Paddy watching. As he stormed away from the tent, he muttered loud enough for them to hear, "Sacred sites and their so-called claims – utter nonsense. This gold rush'll sweep all that aside soon enough."

Jim felt another stab of discomfort. He didn't like Sloane's disregard, but he also couldn't deny his own goal was to find gold, wherever it might lie. Paddy gave Jim a knowing look after Sloane passed. "That bloke's got his sights on Halfmoon Waterhole. Sounds like that's exactly where we ought to go, eh?"

Jim frowned. "If it's on a native reserve, Pat, we could get in strife."
Paddy shrugged. "Plenty of fellas sneak onto 'reserves' after sundown. The troopers can't watch everywhere. And you heard him – he reckons there's gold. You want to be poor forever, or do you want to chance it?"

Before Jim could answer, it was their turn at the warden's table. They quickly registered a two-man prospecting party, nominally for an area "east of Jones Creek." Neither mentioned Halfmoon Waterhole openly. Papers in hand, they stepped away, hearts thumping with excitement. It felt as though they'd just received a secret treasure map.

They spent what little money they had on provisions: flour, tinned bully beef, a coil of rope, extra canteens, and a small cask of precious water. Outside the supplier's tent, Sloane stood talking in low tones to a rough-looking man carrying a rifle – one of his henchmen, perhaps. They fell silent and eyed Jim and Paddy as the pair loaded their goods onto their horses. Jim offered a friendly nod, but Sloane only gave a curt tip of his hat. The henchman spat tobacco juice into the dust.

"Best of luck out there," Sloane said flatly. "Careful you don't get lost. A lot of folk disappear in the bush." There was no mistaking the warning in his voice.

"Thanks for the concern," Paddy replied lightly, "but we can handle ourselves." He patted the long-handled shovel strapped to his saddle as if it were a weapon. Sloane's moustache twitched in irritation.

With everything secured, Jim and Paddy mounted up. They guided their horses eastward, leaving behind the noise and heat of Kalgoorlie's tent city. As they passed the edge of town, they saw the old Wongi elder again. He was seated on the red earth now, smoking a clay pipe and gazing out toward the flat horizon. Jim raised his hand in farewell. The elder watched them silently, the pipe's smoke curling around his deeply lined face.

Once the town receded behind them, the overwhelming silence of the outback enveloped the two prospectors. The land was flat and sparsely vegetated with hardy mulga shrubs and spinifex clumps. In the distance, low hills shimmered in the afternoon heat haze. The track they followed was faint, a mere suggestion in the gibber plain, marked occasionally by a scrap of rag tied to a bush by some previous traveller.

Several miles on, they came upon a lone gnamma hole – a natural depression in a granite outcrop where rainwater collected. Someone had placed pieces of wood over it to slow evaporation. Paddy lifted them and whooped softly upon seeing a small pool of water beneath. They watered their horses and refilled canteens.

"This might be the last sweet water we see for a while," Jim murmured. He noticed hoof prints around the hole – likely others had stopped here, maybe even Sloane or his man ahead of them.

They pressed on as the day cooled and the sky burned orange. After sunset, under a canopy of startlingly bright stars, they made camp. A meagre fire crackled in the stillness, its light dancing on their faces. Dingoes– or perhaps wild dogs – yipped somewhere far off. Paddy tore a chunk off a damper loaf and chewed thoughtfully.

"D'you think there's truth to it, Jim? That the waterhole's cursed or sacred or such?" he asked, staring into the fire.

Jim fed a twig to the flames and considered. He remembered the elder's penetrating gaze. "The Wongi have been here forever. If they say a place is special, I'd wager they have their reasons. Whether it's spirits or just that it's kept them alive in hard times, it's not for us to dismiss."

Paddy nodded slowly. "Aye. But gold… gold doesn't heed spirits. If it's there, someone will dig it, be it us or Sloane or whoever. I just hope we're not stepping into something best left alone."

Jim managed a grin. "Now you're sounding like an old bush yarn. Next, you'll say the bunyip of the billabong will get us."

Paddy chuckled, easing the tension. "Could be a min-min light leads us astray. Or a yowie snatches our supper."

They laughed quietly, trading folklore they'd heard – a necessary balm against the vast unknown darkness around them. Yet when the laughter faded, Jim felt that uneasy prickle again. Perhaps it was only the weight of the stars above, or the absolute silence of the land after their voices ceased. Either way, he found himself murmuring a small prayer before he rolled into his swag for the night: "Keep us safe out here."

Not far from their camp, unseen by the two friends, a dark figure stood on a low rise. Moonlight silhouetted the lean form of a man – Sloane's rifle-toting henchman. He watched the distant glimmer of their campfire for a long moment, then slipped away into the night, heading east.

CHAPTER 2:
WHISPERS AT THE WATERHOLE

By dawn, Jim and Paddy were on the move again, driven by anticipation and a hint of ambition, they pushed forward, eager for what lay ahead. They navigated using a rough sketch map Paddy had drawn from descriptions overheard in the pub – a line for a creek bed, an "X" for Halfmoon Waterhole, and a shaded patch where "rich dirt?" was noted. The country grew more rugged as they went on. Dry watercourses snaked through low hills of ironstone. Occasionally, they saw broken tools or rusted tin cans – signs that other prospectors had passed this way, though none stayed long in such unforgiving terrain.

Near midday, they crested a rocky ridge and finally saw Halfmoon Waterhole below: a crescent-shaped depression fringed by a stand of pale-trunked gum trees. Even from a distance, they could see a shimmer of water at its centre – a rarity that made the spot precious to man and beast alike. Jim's thirst sharpened at the sight.

But something else caught their eyes: near the waterhole stood an abandoned prospectors' camp. Two canvas tents sagged listlessly, and one partially collapsed. A shovel was stuck blade-first in the soil, and scattered about were a few utensils and an overturned crate. The camp looked recent yet deserted.

Paddy frowned. "Could be those fellas we heard about – the O'Keefe brothers. Someone in town said they'd headed this way a fortnight ago." He clicked his tongue. "No sign of them now."

They approached warily. Jim dismounted and called out, "Hello the camp!" His voice echoed against the rocks and died. No reply.

The place felt eerily still. The only sounds were their horses snorting and the incessant drone of flies now gathering around the camp. Jim tied his horse to a branch and stepped closer. A billy hung blackened over a dead fire pit, half-filled with stagnant water and drowned insects. He crouched by the tent flap and peered inside – bedding tossed about, personal belongings strewn. It was as if whoever stayed here left in a hurry…or never returned at all.

Paddy, meanwhile, ventured to the waterhole's edge. The pool of water in the crescent hollow was shallow and silty. On its banks, the mud was churned with hoof prints – camels or horses – and…he knelt, brow furrowed. "Jim, come take a look at this," he called.

Jim joined him and saw what Paddy pointed out: footprints of bare human feet pressed in the mud. Several sets, it looked like, coming and going. Some smaller prints could be Aboriginal – perhaps women or children given the size – and others possibly belonging to European boots that had lost their soles (many prospectors ended up barefoot as boots disintegrated). The tracks overlapped and were partially dried. It was hard to tell how old they were.

"Maybe the O'Keefes had some Wongi guides or visitors?" Jim speculated softly. Aboriginal people sometimes visited camps, either out of curiosity or to trade dingo scalps and kangaroo skins for tea and flour.

Paddy looked around uneasily. At the far side of the pool, under a spreading gum tree, lay something pale. They walked over – it was a shirt, torn and ground into the mud. Dark stains of blood marred the fabric. Nearby, a set of heavy bootprints led toward a cluster of rocks…and simply stopped.

Jim and Paddy exchanged alarmed glances. Boot prints ending abruptly, a bloodied shirt abandoned – it told a grim tale. Paddy quietly drew a long-bladed knife from his belt, and Jim cocked the revolver he carried in his saddlebag.

They followed the boot trail to the rocks. There, in a shaded crevice, flies buzzed frantically. Jim's stomach turned as they discovered the source – a body wedged between boulders, face-down. He recognised the flannel shirt and matted red hair: it was Finn O'Keefe, one of the brothers.

He reached out and gently turned the body over. Finn's eyes stared lifelessly at the sky, mouth open in a final gasp. There was a deep bruise around his neck and scratches across his chest, as if from some struggle. No obvious bullet or knife wounds. It almost looked like he'd been strangled or crushed.

Paddy murmured an oath and crossed himself. "What in God's name happened to him? Where's his brother?"

They searched the area, calling out for the other O'Keefe brother, Sean. Only silence replied. In Finn's stiff hand they found a scrap of damp paper. Jim pried it loose; it was a crumpled note with scrawled writing, barely legible: "…warned not to touch…gold here cursed…Wongi say demon…Wunambi –" the rest was smeared with mud and unreadable.

"Wunambi?" Paddy whispered, perplexed by the strange word. Neither had seen it before.

Jim's pulse quickened. Warned not to touch gold here cursed...Wongi say demon Wunambi... The note was like the ravings of a frightened mind, but here Finn had scrawled it in his final moments. It was clearly meant as a warning or record.

"We need to find Sean," Jim said, jaw set. Whether alive or dead, they couldn't just leave him.

They spent the next hour circling outward from the waterhole, searching every gully and thicket. They found an old coolamon (a wooden bowl) near a tree – likely left by Aboriginal travellers – but no other sign of Sean O'Keefe. What they did notice, however, were additional tracks leading off eastward: prints of boots alongside camel tracks. It seemed someone – possibly Sloane's henchman with a camel – had recently been here too, perhaps after whatever tragedy befell the O'Keefes.

Exhausted and unnerved, Jim and Paddy paused back at the abandoned camp to take stock. They wrapped Finn's body in a canvas groundsheet and moved it into the shade for the time being. Paddy uncovered a small cache of belongings the brothers had stashed: a half-empty bottle of whiskey, a diary too soaked to read, and a pouch containing a few rough gold nuggets, caked with quartz. Paddy's eyes widened at the sight of the gold. "So they did find something."

Jim picked up one nugget, feeling its weight. It was coarse but hefty – perhaps a few ounces. The O'Keefes had struck pay dirt out here after all. But at what cost? He recalled the blood-stained shirt, the chilling note. "Paddy, I've got a bad feeling. Something went very wrong for them... maybe a fight over gold, or maybe—" He didn't finish the thought that maybe the Aboriginal warnings had merit.

"Or maybe Sloane's man found them and wanted their find," Paddy completed grimly, voicing Jim's other fear. There were tales of claim jumpers who wouldn't hesitate to kill lone prospectors for gold. Law out here was thin, and greed sharp.

They decided to return to Kalgoorlie to report this incident, hand over the gold and report the find to the police. It was late afternoon by now; travelling in the cool of evening might be safer. But first, they needed water and rest.

They led their horses to the waterhole to drink. The animals were skittish, rolling their eyes and snorting as they approached the muddy pool. Jim had to tug firmly to get his mare to drink. "Easy girl, easy...we're leaving soon," he whispered, stroking her neck. The horse's ears pinned back; she seemed to sense something Jim couldn't see.

As they refilled their canteens, a sudden chill breeze rippled the water's surface. Jim looked up. The gum trees were still; the breeze came from the earth itself, swirling dust across the pool for an instant. He felt the fine hairs on his arms rise. Paddy cursed softly and stepped back, spilling some water. "Came out of nowhere, that wind."

They heard a faint sound then – a low moan or growl, hard to tell – carrying over the rocks. The horses jerked their heads up, nostrils flaring. Jim instinctively reached for his revolver. But the sound was gone as quickly as it came.

"Could be a dingo," Jim said, attempting to sound unconcerned.
"Let's hope it's not a ghost," Paddy replied half-jokingly, though his smile was forced. He patted Finn's wrapped body. "We should say some words before we go… we might be the only ones to do it."

They buried Finn O'Keefe's body in a shallow grave near the camp, marking it with a pile of stones. Paddy, being Catholic, said a quiet prayer for the dead. Jim bowed his head respectfully. In the dying light, the scene was sombre – two prospectors performing last rites in an empty wilderness, the land silent witness to sorrow.

Unnoticed by them, atop a rocky ledge, a pair of eyes watched their every move. Jandamarra, a young Wongi man, lay on his belly peering down. He had been tracking the movements of the white prospectors since dawn, sent by his elders to keep an eye on the sacred waterhole. He had arrived too late to stop tragedy – the O'Keefe brothers had been beyond saving when he first came upon the scene the day before. Horrified, Jandamarra had sung the lament for the restless spirits, hoping to guide them away. Yet he sensed an immense anger still coiled about this place. The Wongi elders warned that a great mamu, an evil spirit, had been awakened here.

Jandamarra recognised that these two newcomers were not the ones who desecrated the site; that blame he silently placed on the third white man who had crept in earlier with a camel – the one who left hurriedly with something heavy in his bags. Jandamarra suspected it was gold. And he suspected that the Wunambi, the ancient water-snake guardian, had unleashed its wrath because the sacred ground had been defiled by blood and greed. The elders' warnings echoed in his mind: If the ground is made thirsty with blood where it should only drink rain, the spirit will strike back.

He watched Jim and Paddy bury the dead man. That at least was a respectful act. They seemed shaken and not hostile, unlike others who might have blamed his people immediately for such deaths. Even so, he dared not reveal himself yet. There was too much tension. Instead, he resolved to slip back to his own camp tonight and inform old Marnda, the wise woman, what had happened. Perhaps she would know how to appease Wunambi's anger before more lives were lost.

Below, Jim and Paddy finished their grim task. The sun had dipped and the sky was bruised purple in the east. They quickly packed the O'Keefes' few effects – planning to hand them to the authorities – and mounted their horses to head back west. The prospect of riding through the darkness spooked them, but staying here longer felt worse.

As they departed Halfmoon Waterhole, Jim felt a peculiar heaviness in his chest. He took one last look at the shimmering pool of water reflecting the twilight. It appeared placid now, but he could not forget the uncanny breeze or the terror that must have seized Finn when he wrote that note. Wunambi… The name looped in Jim's mind with each hoofbeat.

Night fell fully as they rode on. A crescent moon gave some light, and they navigated by the stars and the faint wagon trail. Both men were silent and alert, senses sharpened by fear. They half-expected Sloane's armed man or some phantom of the desert to leap out from every shadowed boulder.

Several hours later, exhausted and dusty, they saw the distant glow of Kalgoorlie's lights. Relief washed over Jim – civilisation, such as it was, meant safety and help. They urged their tired horses forward.

Yet as they finally approached the edge of town, a piercing wail cut through the night air behind them, from far out in the bush. It was a long, mournful cry that rose and fell – not quite animal, not quite human. It sent a shiver through both men. Jim twisted in his saddle to glance back at the dark horizon. Nothing but blackness and distant stars. He felt that weight in his chest again, like a warning.

Paddy crossed himself once more. "Mary protect us…What was that?" he whispered.

Jim had no answer. He nudged his horse onward. "We'd best find the constable. Quickly." Behind them, the strange wail faded, but neither would forget that sound for a long time to come.

CHAPTER 3
WUNAMBI

They found Senior Constable Daniel O'Ryan at the Kalgoorlie police camp – a cluster of iron sheds and holding cells near the centre of town. O'Ryan was a stout, middle-aged officer with a bristly moustache and a reputation for fairness. He listened gravely as Jim and Paddy, still dust-caked and shaken, recounted their discovery at Halfmoon Waterhole. On the desk between them lay Finn O'Keefe's pouch of gold and the sodden note with the word "Wunambi" visible. O'Ryan picked up the note, brow furrowed.

"You're sure the other brother wasn't there? Sean O'Keefe?" O'Ryan asked.

"Not that we could find, sir," Jim replied. "If he survived whatever happened, he might be wandering out there or taken by someone."

O'Ryan exchanged a glance with a younger constable present. "We'll organise a search at first light. The O'Keefe boys... good lads. Deserved better." He then eyed the gold pouch and note again. "This talk of a curse and... Wunambi. Either of you know what that means?"

Jim shook his head. Paddy offered, "It might be some native word. Finn wrote that they were warned by the Wongi. Maybe 'Wunambi' is what the locals call an evil spirit or demon."

The younger constable, Jack Mercer, spoke up. "I've heard tales from some of the native trackers. They talk about a big snake spirit in these parts, guards waterholes. They're afraid of it."

O'Ryan tapped the note. "Could be the O'Keefes were frightened by local superstition. But something real killed Finn O'Keefe. Strangled, you say, and no sign of the brother. That doesn't sound like a snake attack or any animal. Sounds like a person's work." His expression hardened. "Possibly that person Mr. Sloane and his ilk. I've had my suspicions about him for a while – always skulking about where he's not supposed to be."

Jim felt a measure of vindication that O'Ryan was already considering Sloane. "We saw Sloane's man out there, or signs of him. Camel tracks alongside boot prints. And Sloane was arguing with the warden about that very place."

Mercer nodded. "Sloane has a few hard cases on his payroll. If one of them got wind the O'Keefes found gold, they might've tried to steal it."

Constable O'Ryan stood up, putting on his broad-brimmed hat. "We'll question Sloane soon enough. But first, I'll get a tracker from the native camp and head out with a patrol to look for Sean O'Keefe or any other evidence. Thank you, gentlemen – you've done right by coming to us. Leave the gold and note; they'll be held as evidence for now."

Jim and Paddy agreed though Paddy looked longingly at the gold pouch for a second – their one tangible proof of success. Handing it over to the law meant they might never see a reward for it. But both knew it was necessary.

As they left the police camp, an ambulance cart was being prepared to retrieve Finn's body in the morning. The first hints of dawn's light were showing on the horizon. Jim realised they hadn't slept properly in over a day. Exhaustion tugged at him, but his mind was restless.

"Let's get some rest at my place," Jim suggested. He rented a small room behind a feed store. Paddy was grateful for the invite; the thought of sleeping alone after the night's events unsettled him.

They walked through the awakening town. Market stall vendors were already arranging produce and wares. Bakers stoked their ovens. A few early-rising miners trudged toward the diggings with picks on their shoulders. Life moved on, oblivious to the dark mystery that had unfolded in the wilderness overnight.

As they passed an alley by the Exchange Hotel, they nearly collided with Charles Sloane coming out of a side door, accompanied by his rifle-toting henchman and another man. Sloane's eyes narrowed at seeing them. "Jim Carter," he greeted tersely. "You look like you've seen a ghost."

"Perhaps we have," Jim replied coldly. He wasn't in the mood for Sloane's games. "We found Finn O'Keefe dead. And Sean missing."

For just an instant, Sloane's confident demeanour faltered. "That so?" he said, voice tight. He glanced at his henchman, who avoided his gaze. "Tragic. These goldfields can be dangerous."

"Indeed," Paddy said pointedly, "especially with murderers afoot." It was a bold insinuation, and Jim shot him a slight warning look.

Sloane's nostrils flared. "If you're suggesting something, boy, spit it out plain."

Before Paddy could retort, Jim cut in. "We already reported to the constabulary, Mr. Sloane. I'm sure they'll want to speak with everyone who had interest in that area, including you."

Sloane sneered. "I have nothing to hide. I've been in town all night, ask anyone at the Exchange." He leaned forward, voice lowering. "But mark my words: you go poking where you shouldn't – be it cursed waterholes or accusing decent businessmen – you'll wish you hadn't. The desert's not done claiming fools." With that, he pushed past them, his cronies in tow, boots echoing on the wood planks.

Paddy muttered an insult under his breath. Jim placed a hand on his friend's shoulder. "Don't. He's baiting us. Let the law handle him."

They continued on, though the encounter left a sour taste. Sloane had practically confirmed he knew more than he let on. Jim could only hope O'Ryan was as diligent as he appeared in pursuing the truth.

At Jim's tiny rented room, the two men collapsed onto makeshift beds – Jim on a cot, Paddy on a pile of blankets on the floor. Despite the fatigue, sleep came fitfully. Jim dreamed of the waterhole – of a giant serpent coiling up from the depths, its eyes like opals, chasing him through a labyrinth of gold and bones.

He awoke mid-morning to a gentle knock on the door. Paddy was still snoring softly. Jim rubbed his eyes and opened the door a crack. To his surprise, it was the old Wongi elder who he had seen the day before. The man stood with a younger Aboriginal woman at his side. Jim opened the door fully, suddenly alert. "Hello… can I help you?"

The elder's eyes bore into Jim's with an intensity that belied his frail frame. "You found the whitefella dead at Kurunyarra – the Halfmoon Waterhole," the man stated rather than asked. His English was careful, accented, but clear.

Jim swallowed. News travelled fast in Kalgoorlie, especially among the Wongi who observed everything. "Yes. Finn O'Keefe. We did."

The elder nodded sadly. "I am Bulong. This here is Marnda," he gestured to the woman, who looked middle-aged, her hair streaked with grey, eyes gentle but concerned. Jim recognised her as someone who sold handmade bush remedies in the markets sometimes. "She is a healer. We heard bad things happen out on our country. The spirits are very angry."

Marnda stepped forward, holding out a small bundle wrapped in kangaroo skin. "We bring a gift. Protection." Inside the bundle, Jim saw a smudge stick of eucalyptus leaves and a small carved wooden snake figurine.

Paddy had stirred awake and sat up blinking in confusion at the visitors. Jim took the bundle respectfully. "Thank you... but why give this to me?"

Bulong sighed. "Because you have seen Wunambi's anger. You carry it with you now." He tapped his chest. "The spirit doesn't distinguish, once roused. It will strike wadjela (white men) and Wongi alike if not calmed. We wish no more death."

Marnda added softly, "Light the leaves with fire, breathe the smoke. It will cleanse bad bunyip (evil) from you. And the carving of Wunambi will show him you mean respect, should you return there."

Jim felt a slight chill. The elder spoke as if the spirit were unquestionably real and active. And after what he'd experienced, who was Jim to dismiss it? He glanced at Paddy, who was rubbing his face, trying to catch up. "Sir, ma'am... thank you. But what do you know of what happened? Do you believe Wunambi truly...killed that man?"

Bulong and Marnda exchanged looks. The elder answered carefully, "We only know that place is very sacred. Our ancestors sang songs for it. Something bad must have been done. Blood spilled on sacred ground." He looked down, grief lining his face. "When that happens, spirits can become karradjool — restless, vengeful. Wunambi is a great protector, but also can punish if angered."

He pointed eastward, as if he could see through walls to the far-off site. "The Wongutha people say the great water-snake roamed that land when the world was young, and the tracks he made became the creeks and river. The very water at Halfmoon is part of him. If he feels it defiled...there is trouble."

Marnda placed a hand on Bulong's arm to steady him — speaking of these matters clearly distressed the elder. She turned to Jim and Paddy. "Two nights past, even here in town, we heard a cry on the wind. The bardan wongi (spirit-call). Others heard it too. That's why we came — to warn you and to ask you: please, do not go back there. Leave that place alone."

Paddy stood now, respectfully quiet but his brow knitted. "We don't intend to, ma'am. Not after what we saw. But the police might, and others like Sloane. They won't listen to talk of curses."

Bulong's gaze hardened. "Then more will die." He reached into a dilly bag at his side and pulled out a long polished stone blade. For a heartbeat, Jim tensed, but the elder flipped it in his hand offering the handle to Jim – a gesture of trust. "If you *must* go back, take this. Stone from this land, shaped by my father's father. It has old power. Keep it close."

Jim gingerly accepted the blade, marvelling at its balance and the craftsmanship of the flaked edge. It felt ancient – a piece of the land itself. He suddenly felt a rush of responsibility and connection, as if he were being entrusted with more than just an object.

"We will perform a smoking ceremony tonight," Marnda said. "To try and soothe Wunambi. But it may not be enough if the disturbance continues. Tell your constable – tell any who plan to disturb Halfmoon – that it should be left to heal."

"We'll tell them," Jim promised.

Bulong touched Jim's shoulder lightly. "Thank you. Not all whitefellas listen. You have a good heart to bury that man and speak with us. Spirits see that." The elder offered a half-smile – the first sign of warmth – then turned and shuffled away with Marnda.

Jim closed the door, mind buzzing with all he'd heard. Paddy exhaled deeply. "I feel like I just stepped into a Dreamtime story."

"They believe it completely," Jim murmured, turning the snake carving over in his hand. It was simple but evocative – a serpent with jaws open. "And... given what we experienced, I'm not inclined to dismiss them."

Paddy reached for the smudge stick. "Shall we, then? A little protection smoke?"

Jim lit the bundle of eucalyptus leaves with a match. A fragrant, sharp smoke wafted up. They sat quietly, allowing the smoke to curl around them. Paddy even breathed it in and out, eyes closed in an almost prayerful way. Jim followed suit, feeling a strangely calming effect settle over him.

After a few minutes, Paddy broke the silence. "What do we do now, Jim? Constable O'Ryan will search out there. Sloane's likely to cover his tracks or vanish if he's guilty. And there's this –" he tapped the wooden serpent "– possibly an angry spirit to boot."

Jim set the carving and blade carefully on his small table. "We've stumbled into something big, my friend. This isn't just about one claim or two prospectors. It's like all the tensions of this land – the gold, the rightful owners, the greed, the law – are knotted up in this mystery."

Paddy nodded. "A powder keg, ready to blow."

"Exactly. If O'Ryan isn't careful, it could spark violence. Some miners already gossip that the O'Keefes were 'got at by the locals' or such nonsense.

And the Wongi are fearful of being blamed or of their sacred site being invaded further."

Paddy's face fell at that thought. Racial violence was not unheard of on the frontier; many towns enforced unofficial curfews on Aboriginal people, and worse incidents had occurred elsewhere when whites sought revenge for perceived wrongdoing. "Maybe we should talk to O'Ryan again. Make sure he understands to tread lightly."

Jim agreed. "After all, Bulong and Marnda came to *us* – perhaps because they trust us a bit. We can mediate."

Just then a commotion arose outside on the main street: shouting and the sound of running feet. Jim and Paddy exchanged a quick look and rushed out to see what was happening.

On the main thoroughfare, a small crowd was gathering. Two policemen were half-dragging, half-escorting a handcuffed man – Sloane's henchman, the camel rider – toward the police station. The man was yelling slurs and struggling, a gash on his forehead visible. O'Ryan followed close behind, jaw set. It appeared the constable had wasted no time in rounding up suspects. Townsfolk murmured and trailed after, hungry for drama. Among them, Jim spotted Bulong and Marnda at a distance, eyes fixed on the scene.

Suddenly, a rock flew from somewhere in the crowd and struck the handcuffed man on the side. "Murderer!" someone shouted. "Gold thief!" yelled another. It seemed word of the O'Keefe death had spread, and many assumed this ruffian was the culprit.

From the opposite side of the street, another voice rang out, cutting through the din – a deep, commanding voice: "Hold it right there!" It was Sloane. He stood flanked by two other business owners, glaring at O'Ryan. "On what grounds do you haul in my employee like a common criminal, Constable?"

O'Ryan's face was impassive. "On suspicion of involvement in a murder and theft, Mr. Sloane. Clear out of the way."

Sloane's eyes flashed. "This is an outrage. Luke's been at my store all morning, he's done nothing. You're just trying to pin a mystery on an easy target. If you want to question someone, question the savages who roam out there!"

A few in the crowd muttered agreement; others shouted him down. The tension escalated in an instant – some townsfolk siding with Sloane's prejudice, others with the police and fairness. A couple of hotheaded miners glared at a small group of Wongi who had gathered to watch, and one yelled, "Yeah, what about them? Always sneaking around camps!"

Jim felt his heart lurch – this could turn very ugly. O'Ryan raised his arms, barking, "Enough! Everyone disperse – *now!* This is police business."

Before things could spiral, an imposing figure stepped out of the telegraph office onto the boardwalk – Reverend Matthews, a local preacher known and respected by many. "I'll ask everyone to calm themselves!" he boomed in a pulpit voice. "Let the law do its duty. Go on about your day, friends." He caught eyes with a few miners and gave a stern, fatherly frown. The crowd hesitated, shame creeping in. Several people shuffled away, unwilling to challenge the reverend's moral authority.

Sloane, however, was undeterred. "I'll be speaking to the magistrate about this, constable," he spat. "Dragging an innocent man and besmirching my name – mark me, you'll regret it." Nonetheless, he did not intervene further as O'Ryan and his men hauled the henchman into the station.

Jim and Paddy approached just as O'Ryan came back outside to address lingering onlookers. Jim lowered his voice and spoke quickly. "Constable, might we have a word? It's important."

O'Ryan recognised them and nodded, stepping aside with them a few paces. "I'm a bit occupied, lads. What is it?"

Jim glanced around to ensure no eavesdroppers. "We've spoken with some of the Wongi elders. They're very frightened this will spark violence or further spiritual unrest. They believe a powerful spirit is at work – Wunambi – and they beg that people stay away from that waterhole."

O'Ryan pursed his lips. "I'm inclined to agree about staying away, for safety if not spirits. We went out at first light, you know – me and Mercer and one of the native trackers." He removed his hat and wiped his brow, the morning sun already harsh. "We found signs of a struggle, as you did, and tracks that led to some camel dung a few miles off – likely this fellow Luke trying to make an escape. No sign of Sean O'Keefe though. It's possible…he bolted somewhere, or his body's hidden. The tracker was puzzled; he's a good one and usually can sniff things out. It's like Sean vanished."

Paddy looked troubled. "And what do you think happened to Finn? Strangulation? Did you see anything we missed?"

O'Ryan lowered his voice. "Between us, I suspect Finn was strangled with a rope – he had fibres on his wounds – likely by that brute we arrested, under Sloane's orders. But," he added, "that doesn't explain everything. There were also marks… around his ankles. Looked almost like…scales or bands, oddly patterned bruises. Mercer joked it was as if a giant snake had coiled around them. Gave me a chill, it did." The constable shook his head. "Superstition aside, I have to focus on the living culprits. Sloane's man will be interrogated. If we can break him, maybe we find Sean or get confirmation of murder."

Jim decided now to mention Bulong's warning. "Constable, the elders are going to do some ceremony tonight. They truly fear the spirit won't rest. They caution that more people could get hurt if we…if this isn't handled properly. They gave us these, to protect us." He discreetly showed the carved snake and stone blade tucked in his belt.

O'Ryan eyed them with a mix of respect and scepticism. "I have dealt with Aboriginal people enough to know to respect their beliefs. I won't laugh at that. Thank you for telling me." He sighed deeply. "I'll keep a guard around the native camp tonight, ensure no hothead miners seek revenge for phantom crimes. And I'll strongly advise the warden and others to declare that area off-limits until further notice. It already is by law, but I'll reinforce it."

He placed a firm hand on Jim's shoulder. "You two have done plenty. Now get some proper rest and try to put this out of mind. Leave Sloane and his likes to me." With a nod, he headed back into the station.

As the crowd dispersed, Jim spotted Sloane standing near his store veranda, arms folded, staring daggers at the police station. The captured henchman's camel was tied up outside, laden with packs. No doubt evidence within would incriminate Sloane further – perhaps Sean's belongings or more gold. Sloane caught Jim's glance and his expression darkened further, full of malice. Jim quickly looked away.

He and Paddy slowly walked back toward the lodging. The reverend passed by and gave them a polite nod – news of their discovery clearly had spread to him as well. Town gossip would be aflame by noon.

Paddy spoke quietly, "Maybe O'Ryan's right. We should step back now. Let the law and the Wongi handle what they will."

Jim wasn't so sure. "Unless Sean O'Keefe shows up alive, there will always be whispers and unanswered questions. If Sloane did murder them, why did he leave Finn's gold behind? And where is Sean? If he escaped, why hasn't he come in?"

Paddy frowned. "You think something else happened to Sean? Something…not by human hand?"

Jim considered the pattern of bruises O'Ryan described on Finn's ankles, the weird cry at night, and the elder's fervent belief. "I don't know. Part of me hopes Sean ran off scared and will turn up in a few days. Part of me wonders if Wunambi – whatever that is – took him."

Paddy shuddered at the thought. "If that spirit is real, at least the elders are trying to calm it. Perhaps that will be enough."

They reached Jim's lodging again. Suddenly, the young Wongi man who had been watching from the ridge – Jandamarra – appeared from behind the building. He had been waiting for them. Jim recognised him as one of the trackers occasionally employed by the police, but younger than most.

The youth looked around nervously, then hurried over. "I saw you talk with Bulong. I need to talk with you too," he said in a hushed tone. Up close, Jandamarra's face was drawn with worry, but his eyes were bright and intelligent.

"Of course," Jim said, gesturing for him to come inside where they wouldn't be overheard. Once indoors, with Paddy by the door as lookout, Jandamarra spoke rapidly, emotions spilling out.

"I was there. At Kurunyarra – Halfmoon – when the second whitefella died. I saw part of it." He paused, trembling at the memory. "I followed the two – they found gold near the old gum with the carvings. They dug without offering or asking. I... I warned them to stop, but they laughed. Then that other white man came at night – big one with a camel. He fought them. I stayed hidden. He strangled one brother as the other fled. The camel-man chased after into the dark."

Jim and Paddy listened, rapt. This account aligned with what they suspected. "Sean ran off... did he get away?" Paddy asked, leaning forward.

Jandamarra's eyes filled with tears. "I ran after too, quietly. I heard screaming. By moonlight I saw... I saw *Wunambi*." His voice shook. "A huge shadow in the creekbed. It knocked the camel man down – he screamed and ran back bleeding. But Sean... Sean fell. I think the spirit took him into the earth. One moment he was there, the next... gone."

Paddy looked incredulous, but Jim felt a chill certainty that Jandamarra spoke true to his perception. "So Sean might be... dead, dragged under by something?"

"I searched in daylight. Only drag marks into a deep crack in the ground near the creek. I dared not go closer. That place is too dangerous now," Jandamarra whispered.

Jim exhaled slowly. This was a bombshell – confirming foul play by Sloane's man and possibly confirming a supernatural event. "You must tell Constable O'Ryan this. Your testimony could hang Sloane and free your people of suspicion."

Jandamarra shrank back. "No! I can't go to the police. They may blame me for being there. Or they won't believe about Wunambi and call me liar. Bulong said only share what is needed with those who listen." He looked meaningfully at them.

Paddy ran a hand through his hair, overwhelmed. "This is...blimey. Jim, what do we do with this information?"

Jim realized their role as intermediaries had just become even more critical. The evidence of human crime, at least, needed to reach O'Ryan in a credible way. "Jandamarra, if not a formal statement, can we at least tell O'Ryan what you saw regarding Sloane's man killing Finn? Leave out Wunambi if you want. The law needs that to nail Sloane."

The young Wongi tracker considered, biting his lip. "You can tell about the camel-man and fight. Yes. I want justice for that." He hesitated, then reached into his satchel and pulled out a small item – a locket on a chain. "I found this near where the fight happened. It belongs to one of them, maybe the O'Keefes. Give it to police if it helps." Jim conder it: a silver locket likely containing a loved one's photo – perhaps Sean's keepsake.

"We will," Jim agreed. "And... thank you, Jandamarra. Without you, we'd never know the full story."

Jandamarra managed a ghost of a smile. "We all want the same thing – peace on country, no more needless death." He then glanced at the sky through the window. "I must go. Elders need me for the ceremony."

Jim placed a hand on Jandamarra's shoulder, a gesture of solidarity. "Be safe." The young man slipped back out and was gone like a shadow.

Paddy let out a breath. "Well. That confirms Sloane's guilt but also confirms...something unearthly at play."

Jim nodded slowly. "We should tell O'Ryan at least that Luke – the henchman – definitely killed Finn. That will strengthen the case. As for Sean and Wunambi...I suspect even O'Ryan would have trouble believing that fully. But maybe we can mention that Jandamarra saw Sean fall into a crevice and likely die so they stop searching fruitlessly."

"Yes, spare them chasing a ghost. Or a snake," Paddy quipped darkly.

Jim secured the locket safely. "Let's head over before O'Ryan goes off duty or something."

They stepped out and made their way again to the police station. The day was now hot, and the street quieter as people sought shade. At the station, they learned O'Ryan was out following up leads – likely in a meeting with the Mining Warden or magistrate, pushing the legal case. They left word for him that they had crucial new information from an eyewitness and would return in the evening.

The rest of the afternoon they spent restlessly about town, eating a bit of stew at the communal kitchen tent, and checking on the mood. It seemed, for now, major trouble had been averted. Some miners grumbled about "magic" but others dismissed it and focused on their own claims. The Wongi camp on the outskirts remained quiet and guarded by a pair of constables as O'Ryan had promised. Bulong and Marnda were there, preparing fires and herbs for nightfall.

By dusk, Jim and Paddy returned to the police station and found Constable O'Ryan in his office, looking tired but satisfied. Luke, the henchman, had apparently cracked under questioning. O'Ryan recounted, "He confessed to attacking the O'Keefes under Sloane's orders, to get their gold. Claims he strangled one and chased the other off who 'ran into the darkness screaming'. Says he never caught Sean. Might be the truth or he's hiding and killing him too. Either way, we have enough to charge him and implicate Sloane as an accessory."

Jim and Paddy exchanged a relieved glance – Jandamarra's intel corroborated. Jim handed over the locket. "An item belonging to Sean found at the scene. Perhaps to give the family if they have kin. And…Constable, off the record, one of the native trackers did witness what happened. He's shy to come forward formally, but he confirms Luke's story of Finn's murder. He also believes Sean fell into a crevice and died, which might explain why no one found him."

O'Ryan accepted the locket and sighed. "Poor devils. We'll keep an eye out for eagles or signs, but likely you're right – the second one perished in the escapade. At least now, justice can be done. Sloane's been arrested this afternoon – kicking and screaming mind you – and will face court when the circuit judge comes. The whole town's talking of it. Gold theft and murder on the Goldfields – a story as old as gold itself." He looked both grim and gratified.

Paddy asked, "And what of the place itself? Halfmoon Waterhole?"
O'Ryan tapped a file on his desk. "The warden's declared it temporarily closed to all – even surveyors – under an 'unsafe conditions' pretext. In truth, I put in writing that it should be left for the Aboriginal owners as a gesture. Not sure if that'll stick once Perth hears, but for now no one will go there." He offered a wry smile. "Maybe Wunambi will be pleased, eh?"

Jim smiled back. "I truly hope so. Tonight the Wongi are performing a ceremony to restore balance at the edge of town. We plan to observe from a respectful distance if they allow."

O'Ryan stood and stretched. "They will. Bulong told me I should attend as well, and I think I might. I owe them respect – their land saw injustice and blood, and it's right to acknowledge that. Plus," he added with a softer tone, "after what I've heard and seen, I wouldn't mind some spiritual insurance for myself."

That evening, under a sky fretted with bright stars, the townsfolk of Kalgoorlie heard unusual sounds carrying from the edge of the bush. The Wongi camp was aglow with bonfires. Around them, dozens of Wongi people – men, women, children – gathered in a circle, singing in low, resonant voices.

The ancient song in the Wongatha language rose and fell like a heartbeat. Bulong led the chant, staff in hand, as Marnda and other elders tended a smoking fire of sacred leaves.

Jim, Paddy, Constable O'Ryan, and a few other respectful settlers stood a little ways off, watching quietly.

Jim could not understand the words, but he felt their power – a sorrow for the blood spilled and a plea for harmony to return. He remembered Bulong's earlier words: many sacred sites had been lost or desecrated over the gold rush years. Tonight, perhaps one could be saved.

As the rhythmic song continued, Jandamarra stepped forward from the circle with another young man. Together, they lifted a coolamon filled with water, in the water was the reflection of the moon – a perfect white circle. They carefully poured the water onto the ground, toward each cardinal direction, blessing the earth and appeasing the unseen.

Marnda then cast handfuls of aromatic herbs into the flames. A column of perfumed smoke rose. At that moment, a gentle breeze – much like the one Jim and Paddy felt at the waterhole – stirred, but this time it felt warm, embracing. The smoke drifted eastward, toward Halfmoon Waterhole's direction, as if called there.

Bulong raised his voice in a final refrain, the community echoing him. Jim did not know the translation, but in his heart, he understood it as a farewell to anger and a welcome to peace. By the end of the ceremony, tears streamed down more than a few faces – Aboriginal and settler alike.

In the hush that followed, Bulong approached Constable O'Ryan and, in a gracious gesture, painted a white ochre stripe on the officer's forehead – a sign of respect and inclusion. O'Ryan bowed his head, honoured.

Bulong then approached Jim and Paddy. He took Jim's hands in his own old, calloused ones. "Thank you," the elder said simply. "You listened. You helped justice be done in both worlds – the white law and the black law of the land."

Jim felt humbled. "I only hope we did right. I've learned more in these days than ever before."

Marnda joined them, handing each a small woven charm of emu feathers. "For remembrance," she smiled.

Paddy, fiddling gently with the token, managed a grin. "I don't think I'll ever forget any of this, ma'am. Not as long as I live."

As people began to disperse, returning to their tents or homes, the night felt different – calmer, cooler. The weight that had pressed upon the town lifted. Families of both cultures returned to their routines, perhaps a little more aware of one another's presence than before.

Jim and Paddy walked back into Kalgoorlie side by side under the brilliant stars of the Southern Cross. They passed the once-rowdy pub, now quiet at this late hour, and the broad street that earlier had teemed with anger but was now still. A lone didgeridoo's drone could be heard from the direction of the camp, a soothing nocturne.

Paddy took a deep breath of the night air. "Feels clean again, doesn't it?"
Jim nodded. He looked toward the east, where far beyond the darkness hid the waterhole and its secrets. In his mind's eye he pictured the ground where Finn and perhaps Sean lay in eternal rest. Perhaps their spirits too were appeased by tonight's rites, joining the ancestors in the Dreaming rather than wandering in torment. Jim liked to think so.

He then noticed on the horizon a flicker of lightning – silent and distant, heat lightning from a coming storm. It illuminated a bank of clouds, creating the brief illusion of a serpent-like shape across the sky. Jim's breath caught, but he felt no fear – only awe. It was as if Wunambi's form was outlined in that lightning, watching over the land once more, neither wrathful nor wrathful, just *present*.

"Looks like we might get some rain tomorrow," Paddy remarked, following Jim's gaze to the lightning. "That'd be a blessing."

"Yes," Jim murmured thoughtfully, eyes on the horizon. "A blessing." Rain would wash the earth, fill the waterholes, and perhaps symbolically wash away the blood and regrets of recent days.

In the silence that followed, each man pondered the lessons learned. Jim realized that while he had come to Kalgoorlie for gold, he was leaving this episode with something far more valuable – understanding and respect for the people whose land had given so much. Paddy realized that tales of curses and spirits he'd once scoffed at carried truths within them he couldn't deny.

They parted at the crossroads – Paddy headed for a boarding house bunk, Jim back to his little room. They clasped arms in lieu of a handshake, a camaraderie forged in adversity. "Get some real sleep, mate," Jim said. "We've earned it."

"You as well. And Jim… if you ever do want to try your luck prospecting again, I hear tell there's new diggings near White Feather. Less haunted, hopefully," Paddy joked.

Jim chuckled. "Perhaps. After a long rest." In truth, he wasn't sure he'd ever look at prospecting the same way again. The lust for gold had dulled somewhat, replaced by an appreciation that some things – like peace and community – were worth more.

That night, Jim dreamed not of serpents chasing him, but of walking along a creekbed under a tranquil sky. In the dream, an enormous rainbow-coloured snake slid by him in the water, gentle and unthreatening, and disappeared into a deep billabong. On the bank stood Bulong and Marnda, smiling and beckoning him to share a fire. It was a good dream.

When dawn broke, Kalgoorlie awoke to the rumble of thunder. True to prediction, a cleansing rain swept over the goldfields that morning. Red dust turned to fragrant mud, tents got a needed washing, and the spiky spinifex soaked up the moisture. Children – settler and Wongi alike – ran out to play in the warm rain, laughing as their boots and feet splashed puddles on the same earth that had seen conflict days before.

High above, on the rise that overlooked Halfmoon Waterhole far in the distance, an eagle circled, crying out as if in triumph. And below, in the greening heart of the land, the golden secrets and shadows of the past were slowly being laid to rest, washed by rain and reconciled by understanding. The mystery had not only been solved, but in its solving, it had brought a measure of healing between two peoples. In a place built on gold and greed, a moment of unity and respect had shone through – as enduring as the landscape itself.

Outside Jim Carter's window, a silky pear tree – *karlkurla*, for which the town was named – glistened with raindrops. Jim opened the shutter and reached out to let the cool rainwater wet his hand. He felt renewed. In the distance, a faint echo of a didgeridoo's note resonated through the morning air, mingling with the patter of rain. Jim smiled, whispering a quiet thank you to Wunambi or God or whichever benevolent spirit had guided them through the darkness to the dawn.

The Kalgoorlie gold rush would roar on, with all its trials and triumphs, but this chapter – the mystery of Halfmoon Waterhole – would pass into local legend. Some would tell of the lost gold and the murders solved by the courageous actions of a few. Others would whisper around campfires about the wrath of the great snake spirit and how it was finally calmed by the songs of the Wongi. Both versions, in their own way, spoke the truth.

And years later, when Jim Carter recounted the tale to newcomers under the stars, he would always finish with a gentle reminder: "There are riches in this land beyond the gold. Listen to the people who know its soul. Respect the warnings and the whispers carried on the wind. For if you do, you'll find that even in the wildest of frontiers, justice and harmony can prevail – as surely as the rainbow follows the storm."

CHAPTER 4
THE END OF AN ERA

Jim Sullivan had spent half his life chasing gold.
Some men were born to steady work—to farms, storefronts, and knowing where their next meal came from. Not Jim.

He had come to the goldfields in the mid-1890s, as a young man with nothing but a pick, a pan, and the kind of hope that turned men into fools. Back then, Kalgoorlie-Boulder had been a wild place, full of rough men and rougher luck, where fortunes were made and lost overnight.

But times had changed.

By 1910, the dream of the independent prospector was all but dead. The days of stumbling onto rich surface nuggets were gone—any easily accessible gold had been taken years ago. The mines were now ruled by corporations—Kalgoorlie Mining Company, Ivanhoe, Lake View & Star—companies that had steam-powered machinery and deep-lead mining techniques.

Jim had seen plenty of old prospectors disappear—some turned to working underground for the very syndicates that had outcompeted them; others just faded away, dead in boarding house beds or buried in lonely desert graves.

But Jim wasn't ready to be one of them.
So when whispers of a new strike near White Feather reached town, Jim and his longtime mate, Paddy O'Rourke, decided to roll the dice one last time.

White Feather had once been a fleeting boomtown, but by 1902, most of its easy gold was gone. But now, a San Franciscan named Harlan Tate had arrived, claiming that modern American mining methods could revive old ground.

"The gold's deeper," Tate told Jim, as they surveyed the dry, cracked ground of White Feather. "And with the right technique, we can get it."

For a time, it felt like the old days—men blasting rock, finding traces of gold, and campfires filled with the same old dreams of fortune.
But then the deaths started.
A shaft collapsed, killing three men. The funding from Perth dried up. By

early 1911, the diggings at White Feather were finished.

Jim and Paddy had to move on, they heard about Bullfinch, north of Southern Cross. A new mine had opened there in 1909, but Jim had other ideas—gold had to be somewhere beyond where the mining syndicates were looking.

They set out into the backcountry east Leonora, a vast and deadly expanse, chasing a legend of a lost reef, a vein of gold so rich that a prospector named Cooper had supposedly found it—only to vanish without a trace.

Two days into their journey, they found his bones.
His body lay half-buried in the red dirt, his fingers still clutching black and gold nuggets the size of a man's fist. His revolver was rusted, unfired.

Jim knew what that meant.
He hadn't died of thirst. Someone had killed him.
That night, as the fire burned low, Jim had the feeling he wasn't alone. Tracks in the dust. Movement at the edge of the firelight.

And just past midnight—the horses spooked.
They were being hunted.
The next morning, he made a decision—stay and dig, or leave and live.
Jim wasn't ready to walk away.
That was the last time anyone ever saw him alive.

CHAPTER 5
MODERN-DAY

Beneath the big excavator, geologist Clara Hayes checked her readings. She had spent her career chasing mineral deposits, but nothing about this site made sense. The satellite imaging had been clear—something was down there.

A dense, metallic mass, buried deep beneath the red desert sands. It wasn't gold. The readings didn't match any obvious mineral deposits. It was something else.

Something that shouldn't be there.

Clara had overseen enough digs to know that anomalies like this rarely led to anything good. But this? This was different. The readings were too deliberate, too precise—as if something had been left behind on purpose.

Then, the drill hit something hard.

A shriek of grinding metal cut through the dry desert air, high-pitched and unnatural. Sparks flew from the borehole, white-hot shards flaring against the dust-heavy sky.

"Shut it down!" Clara yelled.

The massive drill rig juddered to a stop, its whirring teeth screeching in protest before falling silent. A low hum of tension rippled through the workers as the dust settled, revealing something beneath the sand.

Clara stepped forward, her pulse hammering in her ears.

The excavation team had expected metal, perhaps the remains of an old structure buried beneath the sand. But as the dust settled, something impossible took shape beneath their hands.

A curve of weathered timber. A jagged edge of wooden planks, bleached by time yet unmistakable.

Someone gasped. The machines fell silent.

No one spoke. No one moved.

The excavators abandoned their heavy machinery, grabbing shovels, and brushing away the layers of history with trembling hands. One by one, the workers stepped back, awe-struck, their tools forgotten.

A boat.
In the middle of the desert.

Clara's breath caught. The impossible lay before them—an answer to a question no one had dared to ask.

A wooden boat.
Not shattered beams. Not splinters from a collapsed mine shaft. But a hull. Curved, intact, unmistakably a boat.
The workers slowed, the excavator operators hesitating, confused.
Clara crouched beside the newly uncovered section, brushing away a layer of fine, ochre-coloured sand. The surface beneath her fingertips was smooth, polished by time rather than decay.

A boat.
A goddamn boat.
In the middle of the Western Australian desert.

The hull, warped but surprisingly well-preserved, bore markings in faded white paint. Letters, peeling but still legible.

'The Kookaburra.'
Clara's breath caught.

She glanced back at the satellite scans, then at the metallic anomaly they had originally detected. The readings hadn't lied—there was metal buried down here. But not in the boat.

Beneath it.

Whatever had brought The Kookaburra to this place—whatever had buried it under tonnes of sand—was still hidden deeper in the earth.
And they had just uncovered the first piece of the puzzle.

Clara Hayes crouched beside the wreck, brushing away layers of fine red dust that had accumulated over decades—maybe centuries. The desert wind moaned through the structure, a sound too hollow, too eerie.
Clara's pulse thrummed in her ears.

She ran her fingers over the Masonic seal, the carved lines faint but unmistakable beneath the peeling paint of The Kookaburra's hull. The sand-covered wreck was an anomaly—a ghost from a history that shouldn't exist here.

Daniel O'Rourke crouched beside her, his camera lens reflecting the amber glow of the desert sky. He had been tagging along for the hell of it—a journalist on sabbatical, claiming he needed an adventure, that he was done writing about politics and corruption.

Well, she thought, he got his damn adventure.

"The Masons were everywhere back in the day," Daniel muttered, snapping another photo. "Mining companies, railway workers, even the first government officials. But a ship marked by them, buried in the middle of the desert?"

He shook his head. "That's a whole new level of weird."

Clara studied the wreckage, running through possibilities. The boat had been here for a long time, but how long? The heat and arid conditions had preserved it in ways the ocean never could.

Then she turned her attention back to the metallic anomaly they had originally detected.

"What if the ship isn't the real mystery?" she murmured.
Daniel raised an eyebrow. "You think something bigger is buried under it?"
Clara stood, dusting sand from her jeans.
"Only one way to find out."

Daniel climbed onto the deck, carefully balancing on the unstable wood. His boots kicked up dust, revealing something carved into the deck of the boat.
J.S.
Clara frowned. The initials were deeply etched, the grooves blackened with age.
She traced them with her fingertips. "J.S.?"
Daniel adjusted his grip on the railing, scanning the deck. "Someone wanted to be remembered."

"Or someone wanted to leave a message," Clara murmured.

She climbed onto the deck, the planks groaning under her weight. Inside the wreck, the interior was surprisingly well-preserved, as if it had been sealed beneath the dunes for decades—maybe longer.

A rusted lantern hung from a hook near the wheelhouse, its cracked glass catching the last slivers of afternoon light. A wooden crate, its edges reinforced with metal bands, sat wedged against the forecastle. The nails had rusted to flakes, but the box itself remained sealed.

Daniel kicked at the sand-covered floorboards. "How the hell does a boat this intact end up here?"

Clara exhaled sharply. "Someone put it here."
Daniel gave her a sceptical look. "What, you think someone dragged a ship into the middle of the desert and buried it?"
Clara didn't answer.
Because yes—that's exactly what it looked like.

With The Kookaburra carefully documented and preserved, Clara turned her attention back to what lay beneath.

The satellite imaging had shown a metallic mass, something too large and too dense to be ordinary debris. The boat had been an impossible find on its own, but Clara had the sinking feeling that the real mystery lay deeper.

The diggers worked carefully, the sun beating down as they cleared the last of the sand away.

A dull metallic glint caught Clara's eye.
Not the ship's hull.
Something else.

She stepped closer as the final layers of sand were brushed aside, revealing a rusted metal plate fixed to the side of The Kookaburra.

It wasn't part of the ship's original structure—that much was obvious.
The corroded surface was marked with symbols even older than the Masonic seal. Some were faint, their meaning long lost to time, while others stood out, still sharp beneath the rust.

And then Clara saw it—
This wasn't just metal plating.
It was a lid.

A metal storage box, built directly into the side of the boat, roughly the size of a shoe cardboard box.

Daniel O'Rourke crouched beside Clara, running his fingers along the rusted metal plate embedded in The Kookaburra's hull. His brow furrowed.
"This wasn't put here by accident," he muttered.

Clara nodded, gripping her small pick. "Someone hid something inside."
She worked the tool into the seam, carefully chipping away at the

corrosion. Rust flaked off in brittle shards, exposing the edges of what looked like a sealed compartment.

Then—
A hollow sound.
Daniel met her gaze. "It's not solid."
Clara swallowed, pressing harder.
The metal groaned in protest.
Then—snap.
The lid broke free, releasing a gust of stale, ancient air into the desert heat.
For a long moment, neither of them moved.
Clara hesitated before reaching inside. Her fingers brushed against something coarse, wrapped in oilcloth, stiff and brittle from age.

She exhaled slowly and pulled it out.
The wrapping crumbled in her hands, revealing something hidden for over a century.
And there—beneath the layers of time—was something even more impossible than the ship itself.

Daniel let out a low whistle. "This just keeps getting better."
Clara barely heard him.
Because as she unfolded the first faded document, her pulse roared in her ears.
Coordinates.
Numbers scrawled in precise, mechanical script.
And as she read them, a cold realisation settled in her gut.
These weren't just any coordinates.
They pointed to a location deep in the desert—hundreds of kilometres away.

A place that, according to every official record, did not exist.

Maps That Shouldn't Exist

The more they uncovered, the more impossible the discovery became.
Beneath the metal plate, Clara found a hidden compartment, stuffed with documents wrapped in brittle oilcloth.
She peeled back the layers, revealing old survey maps.
But these weren't just mining records.
The ink had faded, the pages yellowed, but the markings were still clear—detailed survey lines crisscrossing Western Australia's desert.
Places that weren't on any official maps.
Daniel unfolded one of the maps carefully, his fingers brushing across precise, mechanical script. Unlike the surrounding notes, the base markings weren't handwritten.
They were printed.
"This looks… military," he murmured.

Clara felt a chill creep up her spine.
The government had been involved out here. But in what?
Then, she saw it—
Scrawled hastily in the margins in jagged, frantic black ink.
A warning.
"NOT SAFE. THEY'RE WATCHING."
A knot formed in her stomach.
Daniel turned over another sheet, his brow furrowing.
Then, at the bottom of one map, barely visible beneath the dust and decay, he found something else.
A name.
Or rather—initials.
J.S.
Clara's breath caught.
The same J.S. carved into The Kookaburra's deck.
A Vanished Man?
Clara stared at the initials, the weight of history pressing down on her.
Whoever J.S. was, they had left these maps behind.
As a warning.
And then, somehow—
They had vanished.
Or worse—
They had been buried along with the ship.

A Ship Without a Past

The Kookaburra should have been in the harbour logs if it had sailed up the Swan River.

It should have been in the maritime archives if it had been used as a transport vessel along the coast.
But no records.
No naval logs.
No registry.
Nothing.
Clara checked her GPS coordinates.

They were almost 200 kilometres from the nearest saltwater.
In an area that had never seen an ocean in recorded history.
She swallowed hard.
Whatever The Kookaburra was…
It was never supposed to be found.

CHAPTER 6
THE OUTCROP

The desert stretched endlessly around her, a vast, sun-scorched landscape of red and ochre. The heat shimmered over the sand like a living thing, distorting the horizon, but Clara barely noticed.

She had wandered away from their temporary camp, needing space to think. Too much was happening too fast.
The Kookaburra. The Masonic seal. The coordinates leading to an impossible location.
And now ....

She had spotted the outcrop of rocks about a kilometre from the dig site—standing alone like a silent monument to something long forgotten. No tracks. No signs of past camps. Just silence.

It was what she needed. A place to clear her thoughts.
She leaned against the gnarled native tree, its twisted roots gripping the rocky ground, the only thing casting shade in the vast nothingness.
And then—
Something fell.
A dull thud against the dry earth.
Clara frowned and stepped back.

From the tree's branches, something had been dislodged—a small bundle, wrapped tightly in waterproof oilcloth, wedged deep in the fork of the trunk.
A chill passed through her.
She knelt and reached for it, the cloth stiff and cracked with age.
Her fingers worked against the brittle knots, unwrapping it carefully.
And then she saw it.
A journal.

Bound in aged leather, warped by time, but surprisingly intact.
She turned it over, brushing away dirt from the cover. No name. No markings.

She hesitated before opening it, something in her gut twisting.
How long had this been here?

She swallowed and turned the first page.

January 18, 1911
I found it.
The maps were right.
We weren't supposed to see it.
But we did.
They're coming.
If anyone finds this, know that Jim Sullivan tried to warn you.

Clara felt her breath catch.
The name was familiar.
She had read it before.
J.S.
Jim Sullivan.

The maps were right?.
We weren't supposed to see it?. But we did.
They're coming.

At the bottom of the page, written in shaky, uneven script, were two final words:
"Not alone."

A shadow passed over Clara's face as the sun dipped lower, stretching the wreck's long, jagged silhouette across the sand.

Even more disturbing?

CHAPTER 7
THE LEGEND OF JIM SULLIVAN

Daniel was hunched over his laptop, sifting through old records. He didn't look up when Clara stepped into his tent.

"Hey, you should see this," he muttered, scrolling through the historical registry. "There's nothing—no record of The Kookaburra ever being built, commissioned, or owned. Not in any maritime logs, not even as a private vessel. It's like it never existed."

Clara dropped the journal onto the table.
Daniel's eyes flicked to it, then to her face. "Where'd you—"
She flipped it open to the page.
Daniel read aloud.
"January 18, 1911. I found it. The maps were right. We weren't supposed to see it. But we did. They're coming."
His voice trailed off.
Then, in a whisper, he read the last words.
"Not alone."
A silence settled over them.
Daniel exhaled slowly. "Okay. What the hell did you just find?"
Clara sat down, running a hand through her hair.
"This journal belonged to a prospector. Jim Sullivan. He disappeared in 1911, looking for gold."

Daniel frowned. "Never heard of him."

"No one has," Clara said. "That's the point. He vanished—and now his journal turns up bundled in oilcloth and happens to fall out of the only tree for miles around, just when I happened to lean against it.
Daniel leaned forward, his fingers tapping against the desk. "You think Sullivan found something he wasn't supposed to?"

Clara nodded. "And whatever it was—it was important enough to be hidden."
Daniel's gaze flickered to the wreck outside. "We need to go back in."
Clara hesitated.
Something deep inside her told her they weren't ready. Not yet.

Something was missing.
Then she saw it.
Daniel's laptop was still open.
And on the screen—
Was a map of registered land surveys from 1910.
Clara's pulse skipped.
One of the names listed under a temporary mining lease caught her eye.
James Sullivan.
But that wasn't what stopped her breath.
It was the location.
The coordinates next to his name.
They didn't match the ones where *The Kookaburra* had been found.
They were hundreds of kilometres away—deep in the desert.
Daniel followed her gaze, his brow furrowing. "What is it?"
Clara swallowed hard.
"We're looking in the wrong place."
Daniel frowned. "What do you mean?"
She turned the journal back toward him, pointing to the first entry.
"The maps were right."
Clara looked back at the screen.
Jim Sullivan hadn't just vanished.
He had gone somewhere specific.
And if she was right—
His real discovery wasn't in the wreck of *The Kookaburra*.
It was still waiting out there.
Buried.
Forgotten.
Until now.

Clara stared at the map, her breath shallow. The coordinates on the aged pages, as they taunted her, drawing a line between the past and the present—between Jim Sullivan's disappearance and whatever he had found over a century ago.

Daniel leaned back in his chair, rubbing his jaw. "Let's say Sullivan did find something out there. Something he wasn't supposed to. What the hell does that have to do with a boat buried in the desert?"

Clara shook her head. "I don't know. But whatever it is—it wasn't meant to be found."

Daniel's eyes flicked back to the journal, to the warning scrawled across its pages.
"Not alone."

He exhaled. "I don't like this."

Clara smirked. "You don't have to like it. You just have to help me figure it out."

CHAPTER 8
THE FIRST DEATH

The wind had died down. The air was still. Too still.

Clara stepped into Darren's tent, the beam of her torch cutting through the darkness.

And there he was.

Slumped forward, his body rigid, his face frozen in an expression of pure terror.

Daniel ducked inside behind her. His breath caught in his throat. "Jesus."

Clara forced herself to take in the details. No wounds. No blood. Just wide, unseeing eyes staring into nothing.

Then she saw his hand.

His fingers were curled into a death grip, nails embedded in his own flesh—and in his palm sat a gold nugget.

But not just gold.

The surface was wrong—too smooth in some places, jagged in others, like it had been melted and reformed. The colour, even in the dim torchlight, was unlike any natural gold she had ever seen.

She crouched down. Slowly reached out—then stopped.
A strange hum filled the air.
Faint. Barely there.
Daniel tensed. "Do you hear that?"
Clara nodded. It wasn't coming from outside.
It was coming from Darren's body.
Or the gold in his hand.
She swallowed hard, fighting the instinct to run.
Daniel exhaled sharply. "We need to call this in."
Clara pulled her radio from her belt. "Base, do you copy?"
Static.
She checked her phone. No service.
Daniel grabbed Darren's radio from the floor and tried the same. Nothing.
His jaw tightened. "We had a signal a few hours ago."
Clara's stomach twisted. "Something's interfering."
A gust of wind slammed the tent flap open, sending a ripple through the camp.

Daniel took a slow breath. "So what the hell do we do?"

Their options were clear—and neither of them were good either.

Head back to town and report Darren's death. But that meant abandoning the search for Jim Sullivan's coordinates. And something told Clara they wouldn't get another chance.

The only other option was to split from the team. Take only what they need and head deeper into the desert. Follow the maps. Find out what Jim Sullivan had discovered before someone—or something—stopped him.

The air around them felt heavy as if even the desert itself was holding its breath.

Clara met Daniel's gaze. He already knew what she was thinking.

"You want to go, don't you?"

She hesitated.

"We came all this way. We found the wreck. We found the maps. We found…" she glanced toward Darren's tent, her stomach twisting, "something someone doesn't want us to find."

Daniel exhaled. "And if we don't come back?"

Clara looked at the horizon, where the coordinates waited.

"Then we find out why."

Daniel was silent for a long moment. Then he reached for his pack and slung it over his shoulder.

"Then let's go."

She sat alone in their truck, gripping Jim Sullivan's journal, flipping through the brittle pages. The questions clawed at her mind.

- How did a hundred-year-old prospector end up on a boat in the middle of the desert?
- Why was his journal hidden in a tree, away from The Kookaburra?
- Who really was Jim Sullivan? And who was he running from?
- What had he found that was dangerous enough to bury?
- And most of all—why was Darren dead?

The wind picked up as Daniel grabbed his gear. Daniel slid into the driver's seat beside her, his expression unreadable.

No one in the camp noticed when they slipped away—or if they did, they chose to say nothing.

Darren's body was still in his tent, stiff and cold. The men were waiting, hoping the company's emergency response team would send a retrieval team, but no one could call for help.

No phone signal. No working radios.

MinTech had provided top-of-the-line communication equipment, but now, nothing worked.

The satellite phone had been buzzing with static for the last few hours. The radios cut in and out, only delivering broken fragments of words.
It wasn't natural interference. Something was jamming them.
That meant no way to report Darren's death—at least not until they physically returned to Kalgoorlie.

Darren had been fine hours before his death. Healthy. Laughing. Then something had changed.

Clara's stomach tightened. She kept thinking about the gold nugget clenched in his hand. The unnatural way his face had been frozen in terror.
Daniel adjusted shifted in his seat and adjusted the speed of the ute.
"We head east," he said. "Follow Sullivan's maps."
Clara nodded.

There was no way to know what MinTech would do. No way to know if the company would shut down operations, cover up the death, or send more men to replace Darren and pretend nothing had happened.
They weren't waiting to find out.
Their only path was forward.

The sun was an unrelenting force, turning the desert into a shimmering furnace. The temperature soared past 45 degrees Celsius, waves of heat distorting the horizon. Clara wiped the sweat from her forehead as she adjusted her position in the passenger seat.

Daniel drove in silence, his hands gripping the wheel of their dust-covered Land Cruiser, the GPS mounted to the dashboard showing 56 kilometres left until they reached the coordinates.
Then, without warning—
BANG.
A loud metallic clunk. The vehicle lurched violently to one side.
Daniel wrestled the wheel, trying to keep them steady.
Another bang.
Then—silence.
The engine stuttered. The dashboard lights flickered.
And then, as if deciding it had simply had enough—the vehicle died.
The sudden stillness was deafening.
Daniel let out a slow, controlled breath before slamming his hand against the steering wheel.
"Well. That's not good."

Clara was already unbuckling her seatbelt, climbing out into the scorching heat. The ground beneath her boots was like fire. She rounded the vehicle,

crouching beside Daniel as he popped the hood.
A hissing cloud of steam erupted in their faces.
The radiator was cracked.
The fuel pump had completely seized up.
Their satellite GPS still functioned, but their radio signal was gone.
They were stranded.
Alone.
Miles from anywhere.
And no one knew where they were.

On the first day, they rationed their water. They stayed in the shade of the vehicle, only moving at dawn and dusk to check the surrounding area for any sign of a landmark, water source, or road.

On the second day, the heat became unbearable. The water supply dwindled. The desert stretched endlessly in every direction, an ocean of nothingness.

By the third day, hope had started to slip away.
Clara's lips were cracked, her throat raw. Daniel had stopped talking altogether, focused only on survival. They both knew the statistics. Few who got lost in the outback made it out alive without help.
Then, just as the sun began its descent on the third evening—
A distant hum.
Clara barely lifted her head.
Daniel's eyes snapped open.
The sound grew louder.
A shadow passed overhead—a rescue plane.

Daniel shot up, waving his arms. Clara tilted a side mirror, angling it toward the sky, using the last rays of sunlight to reflect a bright glint back at the aircraft.
The plane circled.
Then—
A crackling voice over their emergency radio.
"This is Kalgoorlie RFDS. Do you copy?"
Relief crashed over Clara like a tidal wave.
"We copy," Daniel rasped. "Two people. Alive but dehydrated. Stranded—coordinates transmitting now."
And just like that—
They were saved.
Or so they thought.

CHAPTER 9
BACK IN TOWN

Two days later, Clara sat in her apartment in Perth, a freshly brewed coffee in her hands.

They had been debriefed, given medical clearance, and warned off.
MinTech had sent a representative—a suited man with rehearsed sympathy and the kind of dead eyes that suggested he knew exactly what had happened.

"You've been through a traumatic experience," he said. "We appreciate your dedication, but this investigation is officially closed."
Clara had nodded. She had signed the papers.
But she hadn't given up.
Now, she sat in front of her laptop, cross-referencing every available source.
The deeper she went, the stranger things became.
- Historical records missing: Local archives had no mention of Jim Sullivan's final days.
- Satellite images appeared altered: The Kookaburra didn't seem to have been there a year ago.
- Her own boss warns her off: "Some mysteries are best left buried."

Then—
As Clara delved deeper into the mystery, the impossible began stacking up.
A wooden boat in the middle of the desert was one thing.
But how had it gotten there between 1911, the last know recorded movements of Jim Sullivan and now?
She ran through the possibilities.
A freak flood event? Unlikely.
A military transport gone wrong? No records.
A cover-up? That seemed more probable.
She kept digging.

The first lead came buried in an old 1928 Royal Australian Navy report—one barely legible in microfilm archives in Perth.
It referenced a classified maritime test project conducted far inland— a naval experiment designed to test transport methods for navigating Australia's uncharted underground karst systems, flooded caverns, and aquifers, or even for mapping subterranean water networks. The project was called "Operation Red Tide."

The report listed one prototype vessel—a reinforced wooden-hulled craft designed to traverse water above and below land when necessary.

The vessel's name?

The Kookaburra.

But there was something strange.

After the 1930 budget records, the project disappeared.

No cancellation. No formal shutdown. Just... erased.

Clara's pulse quickened.

A naval experiment—in the middle of the desert.

A ship that was never recorded as lost—but still turned up in the sand, a century later.

A prospector, Jim Sullivan, who had vanished—somehow linked to the site.

She wasn't the only one asking questions.

Because that's when the second death happened.

It was Daniel who first saw the report.

A single line buried in the online archives of a regional newspaper.

"Another worker found dead near remote MinTech drill site. Authorities cite 'unexplained causes.'"

Clara's stomach dropped.

Unexplained causes. The same vague phrasing was used for Darren.

She snatched Daniel's laptop, scanning the article. The details were scarce, but one fact stood out—the worker had been alone when he died. No signs of violence. No obvious injuries.

And in his hand?

Another black and gold nugget.

Clara inhaled sharply. "Someone's still watching that site."

Daniel nodded grimly. "And they want to make sure no one gets too close."

She turned to the microfilm screen, scrolling through the rest of the 1928 naval report.

Operation Red Tide. A ship lost in time. A prospector who had found something he wasn't supposed to. And now, people were dying.

The deeper she dug, the more impossible it became.

Clara wasn't one for conspiracy theories, but her instincts told her there was more to The Kookaburra than a failed experiment.

So she went back to the archives.

This time, her search took her beyond the 1920s.

She pulled up post-World War II government projects—and found something buried deep in declassified British-Australian military records.

1957: Operation Antler, Maralinga. Nuclear testing. 1958: Christmas Island, British H-bomb tests. 1963: Top-secret land surveys in remote WA.

1964: Redacted documents referencing 'unapproved transport trials' near Kalgoorlie.

Clara's heart pounded.

A cover-up that had started in 1928 didn't just vanish.

It had been reclassified, buried, and rebranded.

What if The Kookaburra wasn't just a transport prototype?

What if it had been repurposed?

What if—someone—had used it for something more?

Daniel peered over Clara's shoulder, reading the same reports.

"Clara," he murmured. "This thing wasn't just forgotten."

She swallowed hard. "It was erased."

There was only one way forward.

The coordinates. Jim Sullivan's final mark on the world.

If she was right, there was something still buried out there.

Something worth killing for.

Something that had cost Sullivan his life.

And maybe—just maybe—it was what MinTech was looking for all along.

Clara exhaled, gripping the edge of the table.

"This isn't just about a missing prospector anymore."

Daniel nodded. "No. It's about whatever the hell they found out there."

Clara closed the file.

They had to go back.

But before they could go, Clara needed to know what she was up against.

She had to be sure—because if she was wrong, she wasn't just chasing a lost prospector.

She was stepping into something bigger.

Her fingers hovered over the keyboard as the screen flickered under the harsh glow of the library's microfilm reader.

She had spent hours combing through declassified British-Australian Cold War documents, piecing together a puzzle that shouldn't exist.

- 1958—Christmas Island.
- 1963—Operation Brumby.
- 1964—Operation Blowdown.
- 1965—Unclassified Western Australia Environmental Impact Reports (REDACTED).

Her stomach twisted.

Why would nuclear tests thousands of kilometres away be linked to remote WA?

She clicked on one of the surviving reports, scanning the faded text.

"Unidentified radiation traces found in soil samples at coordinates ██° ██' S, ██° ██' E.
No further analysis is recommended."

The location was within 200 kilometres of Jim Sullivan's last recorded coordinates.

A cold weight settled in her stomach.

What if The Kookaburra wasn't just an experimental vessel?

Clara had nothing but fragments of truth, tangled in a sea of unanswered questions and too many "what-ifs."

What if it had been transporting nuclear waste?
What if Jim Sullivan had uncovered something far worse than gold?

And what if the danger wasn't just buried in the past?

That night, after heading out for dinner with Daniel, Clara returned to her apartment, her mind still racing.

She barely had time to toss her keys on the counter before she felt it.

Something was wrong.

The door was closed, but the lock was different—scratched. The deadbolt didn't sit flush.

Her pulse spiked.

Someone had been here.

Slowly, she stepped inside, flicking the light on.

At first glance, nothing seemed out of place. No overturned furniture. No broken glass. No scattered papers.

But then she saw her desk.

Her laptop? Gone.

Her printed notes? Missing.

Her USB drive with the declassified files? Nowhere to be found.

A cold wave rolled over her.

This wasn't a robbery.

They hadn't touched her money, her jewellery, or her personal belongings.

Whoever had done this didn't care about valuables.

They cared about secrets.

Someone had scrubbed Operation Red Tide from history.

Someone had erased the connection between Christmas Island's nuclear tests and the remote WA coordinates.

And now—they had erased her work, too.

Her hands curled into fists.

She had gotten too close.

And they wanted to make sure she never got any closer.

Clara sat on the edge of her desk, staring at the empty space where her laptop used to be. The silence of her apartment pressed in around her, the weight of the break-in settling like a stone in her chest.

Someone had been here.

They hadn't just taken her notes. They had erased her ability to retrace them.

But they didn't know about the journal or the maps. Those had never left her side—not for a second. She carried them everywhere. Even to the restroom.

Her fingers curled into fists. Whoever had erased The Kookaburra from history wasn't done. Now, they were trying to erase her work, too.

Her phone buzzed.

Daniel.

She picked up, barely able to keep the frustration from her voice. "Someone broke in."

A pause. Then, "On my way."

Fifteen minutes later, Daniel stepped inside, taking one look at the undisturbed furniture before his eyes landed on the desk. His expression darkened. "This wasn't random, was it?"

Clara shook her head, crossing her arms. "They took my laptop, my notes—everything I had on The Kookaburra and Jim Sullivan."

Daniel let out a slow breath. "They didn't want to just steal your research. They wanted to shut you down."

"Yeah, well." Clara squared her shoulders. "They failed."

Daniel smirked, but there was an edge to it. "We need to get ahead of this. If someone's covering this up, they won't stop at a break-in."

Clara nodded. "Which means we need to go back."

Daniel met her gaze. "To the wreck?"

"No," Clara said, shaking her head. "To the coordinates."

The real mystery wasn't just The Kookaburra. It was where Jim Sullivan had gone after he left it behind. And if he had been running from something, they needed to find out what.

Daniel exhaled. "Alright. But this time, we're prepared."

The next morning, they met at a small café at South Beach in Fremantle, blending in with the joggers and dog walkers, as far removed from Kalgoorlie as it's possible to get. She refused to be anywhere predictable.

Daniel already had coffee waiting. He slid a cup toward her as she sat down.

"Alright," he said, voice low. "We need a plan."

Clara nodded, pulling out an old road map of Western Australia. She traced a line with her finger—past Kalgoorlie, deeper into the Great Victoria Desert.

"We avoid the main highways, stay off-grid as much as possible."

Daniel raised an eyebrow. "So no cell service, no backup, and no help if something goes wrong."

"Pretty much," Clara said. "Which means we need satellite phones, a reliable vehicle, and backup supplies in case we're out there longer than expected."

Daniel leaned back in his chair, considering. "I can get the car."

Clara slid a scrap of paper across the table. "This is everything else we need."

Daniel scanned the list.
- Four-wheel-drive vehicle with extra fuel tanks
- Satellite phone & emergency radio

- Compass & physical maps
- Medical supplies
- Non-perishable food & water for at least two weeks
- High-powered torches & emergency flares
- Camping gear
- Basic mining tools

Daniel tapped his fingers against the table. "You expecting to dig something up?"

Clara shrugged. "Jim Sullivan left coordinates. I don't think he just marked them for fun."

Daniel nodded. "Alright. First step—we get a car."

Daniel had a contact in Perth who specialised in off-road expedition vehicles—the kind built for people who planned on disappearing into the Outback.

They pulled into a dusty lot on the outskirts of the city, where rows of beaten-up trucks sat beside heavily modified four-wheel drives.

A lean man in mirrored sunglasses walked toward them, wiping his hands on a rag.

"You looking for a rental or something that won't let you down when you're three days into nowhere?" he asked.

"That's the one," Daniel said. "We need something that can handle deep desert."

The man, Tommy, nodded, leading them past a row of vehicles before stopping in front of a modified Toyota Land Cruiser.

"Extended range, reinforced suspension, and a bull bar strong enough to get you out of trouble," Tommy said. "You're not taking this out for a joyride, are you?"

Daniel handed him an envelope. "No questions, right?"

Tommy smirked. "Didn't hear a thing."

Their next stop was a specialist supply store—the kind that catered to miners, prospectors, and people who planned on staying off the grid.

They split up to cover ground faster.

Daniel focused on food, water, and medical supplies—enough to last them at least two weeks. Clara handled navigation and survival gear.

She picked up:
- A hand-cranked emergency radio.
- Physical maps and a compass—because last time, the GPS had failed.
- A tarp and digging tools. If Sullivan had buried something, she didn't want to be empty-handed.

Daniel met her at the counter with extra batteries, first-aid kits, and emergency blankets.

Clara glanced at the sky as they packed everything into the Land Cruiser. The heat shimmered off the pavement, the weight of their next move settling heavy in her gut.

They were running out of time.

Whoever had erased The Kookaburra from history had already tried to erase her work.

And if they waited too long, she had no doubt—they'd try to erase her, too.

Back at Clara's apartment, they did one final check of their supplies.

Daniel was tightening the straps on his pack when Clara froze.

A black SUV rolled past the building.

Her stomach twisted.

Daniel glanced up. "That's the third time I've seen that car today."

Clara's hands clenched at her sides. "They're watching."

Daniel sighed. "Then we need to move. Now."

Clara nodded. No goodbyes. No loose ends. From this moment forward, they were off the grid.

They grabbed their gear, loaded up the Land Cruiser, and pulled out of the city under the cover of night.

As they left Perth behind, heading east toward Kalgoorlie, Clara glanced down at Jim Sullivan's weathered old journal in her lap.

The final coordinates were burned into her memory.

This wasn't just about history anymore.

It was about survival.

And whoever had tried to erase The Kookaburra from history—they weren't finished yet.

CHAPTER 10
RETURN TO THE KOOKABURRA

The desert felt different this time.

The heat still pressed down like a suffocating hand, and the wind whispered through the dunes as it always had. But something was off—something that prickled at the back of Clara's mind.

She and Daniel had driven through the night, taking the most indirect route they could manage. They hadn't seen another vehicle for hours, and yet, as they neared The Kookaburra, an unease settled deep in Clara's chest.

This time, it wasn't just the mystery of why a wooden boat had ended up in the middle of the desert.

It was who else had been here.

Daniel killed the engine a few hundred meters away, parking the Land Cruiser behind a low dune and throwing a tan tarp over it. It wasn't much, but it was better than nothing. The last thing they needed was to announce their return.

They moved on foot, their boots crunching over dry, cracked earth.

And then they saw it.

The Kookaburra sat as they had left it, half-buried in sand, its faded hull still standing as a relic of something lost to time. At first glance, it seemed untouched.

But as they drew closer, Clara's breath caught.

"Daniel," she murmured.

He followed her gaze.

The sand around the wreck had been disturbed—drag marks, footprints, indentations where something heavy had been shifted.

Not theirs.

Daniel exhaled sharply. "We were the only ones here last time. This... this is new."

They stepped forward cautiously. Daniel pulled out a small flashlight, sweeping it over the wooden structure.

More details emerged.
Freshly broken planks—someone had been searching inside.

The metal storage compartment—once locked, now forced open and empty.
Scattered footprints—a third set besides their own.
Clara's stomach twisted.

Was this just the aftermath of the second worker's death, or was it something more? After everything Clara had seen in the past few weeks, nothing surprised her anymore.

Daniel crouched, running his fingers over a boot print in the sand. It was larger than either of theirs. Heavy-soled. Recent.

"Not just knew," he said grimly. "They got here after us."

Clara turned, scanning the horizon. The sun was dipping lower, the shadows stretching long over the dunes.
Then she saw it.
Something new, carved deep into the deck.
Daniel stepped forward, reading the gouged words.
STOP DIGGING.
The letters were jagged, hacked into the wood with something sharp. The strokes were uneven, hurried—desperate.
A warning.
Or a promise.
Clara swallowed hard, forcing herself to stay calm. "Who the hell left that?"
Daniel shook his head. "The bigger question is—are they still here?"
They both turned toward the desert, toward the shifting dunes, toward the emptiness.
But Clara had been in these places long enough to know…
They were not alone.
The wind picked up, stirring the sand in slow, ghostly waves.
Clara had spent enough time in the Outback to trust her instincts, and right now, those instincts screamed at her.
They were being watched.
She kept her breathing steady, scanning the landscape for movement. Nothing. No signs of life. Just the endless expanse of sun-bleached rock and dust.
And yet, the air felt heavier.
A sudden gust of wind swept through the wreck, making the wooden planks creak, shifting the sand beneath them.
Then, a shadow moved.
Not Daniel's.

Not hers.

Something flickered—just at the edge of her vision.

A tall, elongated figure standing at the crest of a nearby dune.

Clara's breath caught.

For a moment, she saw eyes—deep, watching, and ancient.

The Wunambi.

The rainbow colour serpent.

It was said that when blood was spilled on Country, the spirits lingered, watching, waiting, remembering.

Clara had always dismissed the stories as legends.

But now—now, she wasn't so sure.

Daniel tensed beside her, gripping her arm. "Clara, what the hell—?"

And then it was gone.

Like mist dissolving in the heat.

The air remained heavy, thick with something unspoken.

Daniel let out a shaky breath. "Tell me you saw that."

Clara swallowed, nodding. "Yeah."

A silence stretched between them.

Daniel exhaled, rubbing his face. "You know, I was fine with the missing prospector and the stolen artefact. But this?" He gestured at the dunes, voice tight. "This is something else."

Clara forced herself to focus.

She turned back to The Kookaburra, her heart still pounding.

The storage compartment was empty. Last time, they had left it untouched, its lock intact.

Now, the metal door gaped open, its secrets gone.

"Whatever was inside," Daniel said, voicing her thoughts, "it's gone."

Clara's mind raced.

If they had left it locked, and someone else had broken in…

What had been so important that it needed to be stolen?

She knelt beside the disturbed sand, brushing away loose grains, searching for anything the intruder might have left behind.

Then she spotted it.

A small piece of dark, gold, metallic rock, half-buried in the sand.

She picked it up, turning it over in her palm.

It was unnaturally smooth.

Cold, despite the desert heat.

It shimmered faintly in the dimming light.

Daniel crouched beside her, frowning. "What is that?"

Clara shook her head. "I don't know."

But deep down, she had a terrible suspicion.

Jim Sullivan had marked his final coordinates for a reason.

Maybe he had found gold.
Or maybe…
He had found something far more dangerous.
Something that never should have been disturbed.
Daniel exhaled, looking back toward the horizon.
"You still want to go to the coordinates, don't you?"
Clara's grip tightened on the strange rock.
She nodded.
"Now more than ever."

CHAPTER 11
THE WATCHERS

Clara and Daniel set out at first light, heading deeper into the desert toward Jim Sullivan's last recorded coordinates. The sun rose fast, burning away the early morning chill, and the endless horizon shimmered with heat. They packed light—water, rations, a satellite GPS that had been unreliable at best, and Jim Sullivan's journal and maps.

They were going beyond where any official mining survey had ever recorded.

Daniel was silent as he drove, his fingers tight on the wheel. The unease from their discovery at The Kookaburra hadn't lifted. If anything, it had settled heavier over them, thick as the heat pressing down on the Land Cruiser.

Clara, sitting in the passenger seat, traced her fingers over the piece of dark gold metallic rock she had found near the wreck. She still didn't know what it was—but it felt wrong. Too smooth. Too heavy for its size. And despite being out in the desert for who knew how long, it was still unnaturally cold.

"We should have tested it before bringing it with us," Daniel muttered, glancing at the stone. "Could be toxic."
Clara exhaled. "Could be. But I need to know what Jim Sullivan found."
Daniel didn't argue. But Clara caught the way his jaw tensed, like something was already gnawing at him.
They drove for hours, following the GPS, though it flickered and glitched every so often. Clara checked the old maps, cross-referencing them with their surroundings.
They were close.
Too close.
And then—the temperature changed.
The air thickened.
The cool morning had long since burned away, but this wasn't just the usual midday heat.
This was oppressive.
The temperature spiked suddenly, suffocatingly, unnaturally. The kind of heat that made it feel like the sun itself had drawn closer.
Clara wiped sweat from her brow. The air shimmered, warping the distant

dunes like a mirage.

Daniel slowed the vehicle. "This doesn't feel right."
Clara checked her phone's temperature reading.
It had jumped to 51°C (123°F).
Too fast. Too sudden.
Even for the Outback.
The air tasted metallic, thick on her tongue.
She turned to Daniel. "You okay?"
Daniel didn't answer right away.
His fingers flexed on the wheel.
Then—he swayed.
Clara caught him just before his head tipped forward.
"Daniel!"

He groaned, blinking rapidly. "Shit. I—dizzy."
Clara grabbed his wrist. His pulse raced.

She looked around—nothing but desert. They were still moving, but at this rate, Daniel wouldn't be able to drive much longer.
"Pull over," she ordered.

Daniel barely managed it, stopping the Land Cruiser before slumping back against the seat.

Clara grabbed their water supply, making him drink. "This isn't just the heat."

Daniel pressed his fingers to his temples. "Feels like my brain's buzzing. Like my skull's too tight."
Clara helped Daniel climb out of the Land Cruiser, steadying him as he leaned against the car for support.
He looked at her—then his eyes widened.
"Clara," he whispered. "Behind you."
She spun around.
Nothing.
Just sand.

But Daniel was still staring past her, his face pale.
"You didn't see that?" he murmured.
"See what?" Clara's skin crawled.
Daniel swallowed, gripping the dashboard like he was grounding himself. "Someone. No—something. Standing right behind you."
Clara scanned the horizon.
Empty.
The desert stretched endlessly, just as it always had.
But it didn't feel empty.

Her heart pounded.

She had been feeling something watching them since The Kookaburra. But now? The presence was almost tangible.

Clara turned back to Daniel. His skin was damp, his breathing shallow.

They had to keep moving.

Whatever was here—they had just entered its territory.

As they continued toward the coordinates, Daniel's condition worsened.

The headaches, the nausea, the dizziness.

Clara had seen this before.

Radiation poisoning.

She recalled the declassified Cold War files—Operation Red Tide. The environmental impact reports. The unexplained radiation traces were found near Jim Sullivan's coordinates.

Had they stumbled into an old testing site?

But this felt different.

Radiation exposure caused illness, yes.

But hallucinations?

Paranoia?

A feeling of being watched?

Something didn't add up.

Clara adjusted the GPS. The device glitched again. The signal cut out completely for a few moments before reconnecting.

Daniel grimaced. "Either that thing is broken, or something's screwing with the signal."

Clara checked the compass.

It spun wildly, unable to find true north.

She froze.

Magnetic interference.

She had seen it before—near deposits of iron, nickel, or cobalt. Even volcanic rock could throw off a compass. Some radioactive materials, heavy metals, and naturally occurring rare earth elements could do the same.

Her mind raced through possibilities.

Lodestone? No—too weak.

Uraninite? Possible, but unlikely out here.

Something artificial—an old wrecked transmitter, an underground structure?

Then a thought struck her.

Thorium oxide.
Could that explain everything?

Had Jim Sullivan found a natural thorium deposit—and accidentally unearthed something no one was supposed to see?

By late afternoon, they arrived at the coordinates.
There was nothing there.
Just sand. Empty land. No signs of digging. No signs that anyone—let alone Jim Sullivan—had ever set foot here.

Daniel let out a breathless, disbelieving laugh. "We drove across the desert for this?" Clara wasn't convinced.
She checked the old maps. Jim had marked this place for a reason.
She scanned the area, then pulled out a small Geiger counter.
If this was a radiation site, they would know soon enough.
She switched it on.
The needle jumped.
Clara gasped. "It's here."
Daniel peered at the device. "How bad?"

"Not lethal. But significant." Clara's pulse pounded. "Something is buried here."

They grabbed their shovels and started digging.
The sand was loose at first.
Then, a glint of metal caught Clara's eye, half-buried under the shifting sand.
She stood and stepped forward, brushing away the grains until her fingers met cold, rusted steel.
The sign was old—pitted, corroded—but the message was still clear, stamped in faded red paint:
DANGER. KEEP OUT.
COMMONWEALTH PROPERTY—NO UNAUTHORISED PERSONNEL.
Clara straightened, glancing around. The ground wasn't just sand. Beneath the shifting dunes, something harder lurked—a layer of packed earth mixed with metallic debris.
And then it hit her.
The interference wasn't coming from a single source.
It was everywhere.
She turned to Daniel, voice tight. "This wasn't just some lost shipment. Whatever they were doing here—it's still beneath us."
Daniel looked at her, then at the vast, empty land stretching out in all directions.
He swallowed hard. "And we just walked straight into it."

She glanced back toward the dunes, suddenly uneasy.
Something felt wrong.
Then she noticed.
The wind had stopped.
The desert had gone completely silent.
No movement. No shifting sand.
Not even their own breath seemed loud enough.
Daniel tensed beside her.
And then—
A distant sound.
A deep, low hum.
Faint at first, then growing.
Clara's pulse spiked. "What the hell is that?"
Daniel turned toward the horizon.
And froze.
Clara followed his gaze.
A figure stood on the horizon.
Dark. Watching.
And then—more appeared.
One.
Then two.
Then many.
Shadows stretching across the dunes.
Daniel whispered, his voice hollow.
"We're not alone."

Daniel stopped mid-step, his gaze locked on the horizon.

Clara saw the shift in his expression—unfocused, distant, like he was hearing something she couldn't.

"Daniel?" she asked cautiously.

His lips parted, barely a whisper. "We need to go. We're close."

He started moving. Not running, not panicked—just walking with purpose, like a man following a map no one else could see.

Clara hesitated, then followed.

The sand shifted underfoot, slowing their pace. Daniel barely seemed to notice.

Then, suddenly—he stopped.

Just ahead, the ground dipped into a shallow depression of stone and sand. A gap in the rock.

At first, it looked like nothing—just another break in the desert's endless monotony.

But as Clara stepped closer, she saw the truth.

It wasn't natural.

It was too perfect, too symmetrical.

A cave entrance—half-buried, just big enough for a man to crawl through.

Her pulse quickened. "This wasn't formed by erosion."

Daniel crouched, peering inside. His fingers traced the edge of the opening, where tool marks were barely visible beneath decades of wear.

"Someone made this," he murmured.

Clara swallowed hard, the weight of realisation settling over her like a stone.

"Jim Sullivan," she whispered.

CHAPTER 12
THE CAVE OF SECRETS

The darkness swallowed them whole.

Clara flicked on her torch, the beam slicing through the dust-filled air. The scent of damp earth and old decay settled thickly in her lungs.

The walls weren't smooth like a natural cave. They were rough-hewn, uneven—but unmistakably man-made. The deeper they moved, the more obvious it became.

This wasn't just a cave.

It was a mine shaft.

Something had been buried here.

And then—someone had come back for it.

But Clara knew one thing: dark holes in Australia never stayed empty for long.

Her torchlight skimmed across jagged rock, catching the glistening shimmer of silk. A web stretched between stone formations. A fat huntsman spider clung to the side, its legs twitching, disturbed by the light.

Daniel swore under his breath, stepping carefully. "If I see a snake, I'm out."

Clara wasn't sure he was joking. She kept the beam moving, her pulse quickening. Snakes loved burrows like this—warm, still places where they could coil unseen. If this shaft had collapsed at any point, leaving pockets of untouched air, anything could have slithered in.

Daniel ran his fingers along the rock, his voice tight. "This wasn't just dug out—it was worked. Reinforced. They were extracting something."

Clara exhaled, watching her step as she moved deeper. "And whatever they found, someone wanted it buried again."

The air grew thicker, and cooler. The ground beneath them was uneven, dirt shifting under their boots like it had been disturbed, moved.

Then, Clara's torch landed on something impossible.

A rusted mining cart.

Daniel froze. "How the hell did this get here?"

The cart sat on warped iron tracks, twisted by time. Whatever had once been mined here had been hauled out long ago.

And then—Clara saw something else.

Her breath caught.

A human skull.

The bones were undisturbed, perfectly positioned—as if whoever had died here had never been moved. The skull's empty sockets stared upward, deep and hollow, like they had been watching for something that never came.

She stepped closer.

Her boot scuffed against the ribs.

Something moved.

A dry clicking sound.

A centipede slithered out from between the vertebrae, its long body disappearing into the dust.

Clara shivered but crouched, her fingers brushing against the dirt beside the remains.

An old pickaxe, still clutched in skeletal fingers, rusted but intact.

And something else.

A leather pouch.

She reached for it, brushing away the dust. The leather was fragile, cracking at her touch. Slowly, she pulled it open.

Inside—

A rock. And beside it, a long, polished stone blade. A fragment of the land, shaped by a father's father. It carried old power, the weight of something ancient and unbroken.

But the rock—

No.

It wasn't just a rock.

It was golden—but not quite gold. The surface was flecked with something darker, veins of dull black twisting through the metal like a whisper of corruption. Even in the dim light, it looked... wrong.

Clara's hands trembled as she turned it over.

"What is this?" she whispered.

Daniel leaned in, staring at the rock like it might bite.

"I don't think it's gold."

Clara's mind raced.

This was what Jim Sullivan found.

This was what he died protecting.

And then—she saw one final thing.

A scrap of paper, buried beneath the dust.

Jim's final words.

She picked it up, unfolding it carefully. The ink was faded, the edges brittle.

The message was short.

The writing shaky.

They took it.

It wasn't gold.

I was never alone.

The land remembers.

Clara exhaled shakily.

The land remembers.

Her stomach twisted.

She thought of the shadows in the dunes, the way the wind had stopped, watching them. The way the desert itself had seemed alive.

Then—Daniel swayed.

Clara caught his arm. "Daniel?"

He blinked rapidly, gripping his head. His skin was damp, too pale. His pulse—too fast.

"I don't feel right," he rasped.

The air in the cave thickened.

Heavy.

Like the earth itself was pressing down on them.

The heat should have faded this deep underground.

But it hadn't.

If anything—it was getting hotter.

Clara glanced down at the glowing rock in her hand.

Was this it?

Was this what Jim Sullivan had found?

Then—a noise.

A whisper.

Not wind.

Not rock shifting.

Something else.

Something inside the cave with them.

Clara swung her torch around—nothing.

But the feeling of being watched pressed down on her like a weight.

Daniel shuddered. "We need to leave."

Clara wasn't about to argue.

She stuffed the rock back into the pouch, tucking it into her pocket. She grabbed Jim's final message, folding it carefully.

They turned for the exit.

And then—

A shadow moved.

Not behind them.

Not along the walls.

But from the bones.

Clara froze.

The darkness rippled, shifting—something rising from where the corpse lay.

At first, it was just a distortion, like heat waves on the horizon.

But then—it took shape.

Too tall. Too thin. Too wrong.

Daniel's breath hitched. "Did you see—"

Clara yanked him forward.

They ran.

They burst into the open desert, the heat slamming into them like a physical force.

Clara gasped for air.

Daniel staggered, bracing himself against the rock.

Then—the sound followed them.

A deep, low hum.

Clara turned sharply.

The air above the cave shimmered.

Like a mirage.

Or like something standing there—watching.

Her pulse pounded.

Jim Sullivan's words echoed in her head.

I was never alone.

The land remembers.

Clara turned to Daniel. "We can't stay here."

He nodded, still pale. "We take what we found. We figure out what this is."

Clara pulled the pouch from her pocket, feeling the cold weight of the strange black and golden rock.

Whatever it was—Jim had died for it.

And now—so had others.

The sun dipped toward the horizon, casting the desert in long, stretching shadows.

And as they drove away, kicking up dust and sand in their wake—

Clara could have sworn she saw someone standing at the mouth of the cave.

Watching them.

CHAPTER 13
WHAT NEXT

By the time they reached the outskirts of Kalgoorlie, the air felt lighter. The pressure had lifted.

Daniel parked the Land Cruiser outside a small motel on the edge of town. They needed to regroup, while they figured out their next move.

Clara wasted no time. She spread their findings across the motel bed—Jim's journal, his final message, the pouch containing the strange mineral.
Daniel sat heavily on the mattress, rubbing his temples. His headache hadn't faded.

Clara pulled out her phone, searching for any mention of similar materials.
The results sent a chill through her.
A single, obscure geological report from the 1950s.
A possible unknown mineral deposit was found deep in Western Australia.
The location?
Less than 30 kilometres from Jim Sullivan's cave.
Clara turned to Daniel, her voice hushed.
"This wasn't just gold."
Daniel exhaled. "No. It was something else."
Something the land remembered.
Something it wasn't willing to give up without a fight.

They weren't done yet.
Something had been taken from Jim Sullivan.
Something had been buried in the desert for a reason.
And now, more than a century later—
Clara and Daniel had dug it up again.
The real question was—
Would they live long enough to find out why?
The room was silent except for the sharp, erratic click-click-click of the Geiger counter.

Clara and Daniel stared at the strange black and gold rock, now resting on the motel bed, bathed in the dim glow of the bedside lamp.

Clara adjusted the settings, running the device over it again.
The clicks spiked.
Enough for concern but not dangerously high.

Daniel leaned back in his chair, rubbing his temples. "Jesus."
Clara exhaled. "It's not gold."

She picked up the pouch, gripping the brittle leather in her hands. "Jim Sullivan didn't find gold."
Daniel's eyes darkened. "I think he found thorium dioxide."
They both knew what that meant.

What if Jim Sullivan had stumbled upon something far more valuable—and far more dangerous?
A natural deposit of THO_2, hidden deep beneath the Western Australian desert.
Something that had been buried for a reason.
Something that someone had been covering up for over a century.
And now—they knew too much.

Daniel stood abruptly, pacing the small motel room.
"Okay," he said, running a hand through his hair. "This explains... a lot."

Clara sat on the edge of the bed, staring at Jim's journal—the only entry, the only words he left behind.
They took it.
It wasn't gold.
I was never alone.
The land remembers.

She exhaled. "Jim didn't leave much, but he left this." She tapped the page. "We thought he was talking about gold. But what if he found something else?"

Daniel slowed, rubbing the back of his neck. "Okay, but how does that explain the Kookaburra? That boat wasn't exactly built for dry land."
Clara frowned. "I don't think it was always dry land."
Daniel looked up. "You think there was water here?"
Clara nodded, leaning forward. "The area around the wreck is strange. The ground doesn't match the rest of the desert. And the deposits—whatever they are—are spread out, not concentrated. That wouldn't happen if this was just a buried mine."

Daniel exhaled sharply. "You're saying this wasn't a dumping ground. It was fallout?"
Clara hesitated. "Maybe. But from what? There's no record of testing

here."

Daniel sat down heavily, shaking his head. "That we know of."

Silence stretched between them.

Jim's words loomed in the dim motel light.

I was never alone.

Daniel tapped his fingers against the table. "So. We've got an abandoned boat, a missing prospector, deposits that shouldn't be here, and a journal that sounds like a warning."

Clara's stomach twisted.

"The land remembers," she murmured.

Daniel met her gaze.

"Yeah," he said quietly. "And whatever happened here, it isn't done with us yet."

Except the secret wasn't dead.

Not anymore.

Clara sat on the edge of the bed, eyes locked on her laptop screen.

Daniel paced behind her, running a hand through his hair.

"We're missing something," he muttered. "MinTech wouldn't risk all this for just iron ore. And thorium isn't exactly a billion-dollar trade in Australia."

Clara nodded. "Then what are they doing with it?"

She scrolled through the shipping records again, cross-referencing MinTech's declared exports with actual weight loads.

Then, she saw it.

A shipment from Port Hedland, one of the largest bulk export terminals in Australia. Destination: Qingdao, China.

Official cargo? Premium-grade iron ore.

Daniel frowned. "That's normal, isn't it? Western Australia exports iron to China all the time."

Clara leaned in, eyes narrowing. "Look at the weight."

Daniel stepped closer.

The tonnage didn't match.

MinTech had declared the cargo at a lower density than standard hematite ore—but if it was mixed with something else, like processed THO_2, the numbers would make sense.

Daniel exhaled sharply. "Huh."

Clara's pulse pounded. "They're cutting thorium oxide into iron ore shipments. That way, it won't raise suspicion."

Daniel sat down heavily, shaking his head. "That means China's already buying it."

They stared at each other.
This wasn't just a mining scandal.
This was international smuggling on an industrial scale.

CHAPTER 14
MINTECH

The boardroom on the 52nd floor of MinTech's headquarters had been built for control. Floor-to-ceiling windows overlooked the Perth skyline, a quiet reminder of the empire that had grown from the ground beneath them.

Christopher Fayes, Director of Strategic Operations, stood at the head of the long glass table, watching his executives.
They were nervous.
The news had come in twenty minutes ago.
The journalists weren't dead.
And worse—they weren't running anymore.

"They had somehow found the shipping manifests," said Teah Glance, Chief Counsel. She sat stiffly, her manicured fingers drumming against her tablet. "They have enough to link the Port Hedland operations to the Qingdao shipments."
Silence.
Across the table, Michael Taines, the company's CEO, exhaled. "That's bad."
Christopher didn't reply. He knew exactly how bad it was.
The iron ore shipments had been their greatest cover—no one questioned Australian iron going to China.
Until now.

"This shouldn't have happened." David Conder, Head of Security, spoke gruffly. "We neutralised Sullivan's legacy years ago. No trace left."
Hayes glanced at him. "You thought."
Conder' jaw tightened.
Fayes turned back to the room. "Daniel O'Rourke is a journalist. Clara Hayes was an unknown, but she's proved... resourceful."
He tapped the tablet in front of him. It displayed a CCTV still from Kalgoorlie—grainy but clear enough.
Daniel and Clara.
Still alive.
Still investigating.
Taines leaned forward. "They haven't gone public. Why?"
Fayes smirked. "Because they're not ready."
He paced slowly, hands clasped behind his back.

"They don't just want a story. They want proof. Which means…"

"They're coming here." Glance finished his thought.

A beat of silence.

Then, Conder chuckled.

"Let them come."

"Gentlemen," Hayes continued smoothly, "MinTech is too big to fall over a single headline. But if this reaches the wrong people before we control the narrative…"

He let the words hang in the air.

Glance spoke first. "Then we get ahead of it."

Teah Glance set her tablet down with a quiet click, eyes scanning the room.

"This situation is escalating." She spoke evenly, but the tension in her jaw was unmistakable. "Our people have identified Haye and O'Rourke. They're in Perth. They've already accessed classified shipping data."

Christopher Hayes, Director of Strategic Operations, leaned back in his chair. "Then we shut them down."

David Conder, Head of Security, exhaled sharply. "And how exactly do you propose we do that? They're not stupid. O'Rourke's a journalist—he's got contacts. If he gets even a fraction of this story out, we'll have every regulatory body breathing down our necks."

Taines, the CEO, rubbed his temple. "We have leverage. Money talks. Make them an offer."

Glance shook her head. "That works with employees, not with journalists."

Hayes steepled his fingers. "Make it big enough, and they'll listen."

"Or," Conder interjected, "it just confirms that they're onto something valuable. They won't take a settlement; they'll smell blood in the water."

A silence settled over the table.

Glance finally sighed. "Alright. We have three options."

She turned to her assistant, who immediately pulled up a contingency document onto the room's sleek display screen.

Option One: Buy Them Off.
- Offer Hayes a severance package—enough to tempt, but legally binding.
- A full NDA, barring them from speaking another word.
- A quiet offshore position for Daniel, something lucrative but distant.

"That's our first move," Taines said firmly. "We offer them a way out—money, security, no loose ends."

"And if they don't take it?" Conder asked, arms crossed.

Glance didn't hesitate. "We destroy them."

She tapped the screen, bringing up the second file.

Option Two: Public Discrediting.
- Leak fabricated intelligence ties between O'Rourke and a foreign government.
- Plant fraudulent research misconduct on Carter's record—make her a liability in professional circles.

Taines adjusted his glasses. "If they're discredited before they go public, no one will believe them."

Conder smirked. "That's better. We kill the story before it even starts."

Fayes nodded slowly. "It's a solid strategy. But let's be clear: If we do this, it's a full-scale takedown. Once we go down this path, there's no walking back."

Another pause.

Glance sighed. "Then there's Option Three."

The display switched to the final contingency plan.

Option Three: Erasure.
- No media scandal. No loose ends.
- A staged accident. A missing person. A body never found.
- Make it look like they were never here, lost in the desert, like many a foolish prospector.

A quiet tension filled the boardroom.

For a long moment, no one spoke.

Then Conder leaned forward. "Let's not pretend like we haven't handled things this way before."

Glance shot him a sharp look, but Fayes only smiled.

"True," Fayes admitted. "But they're already in too deep. If we go straight to Option Three, it raises the risk profile. Accidents are messy."

Taines cleared his throat. "Option Two is the safest. No blood, no bodies, no press scandals."

Conders shook his head. "Discrediting works on nobodies. O'Rourke has a reputation. Hayes's got nothing to lose." He leaned back, voice turning cold. "If we want certainty, we make them disappear."

Fayes considered the options for a moment, watching the nervous glances exchanged around the table.

Then, slowly, he straightened.

"We try Option One," he said, voice final. "We make them an offer."

A brief silence.

"And if they refuse?" Conder asked.

Fayes met his gaze.

"Then we bury them."

Fayes smirked.

"I prefer they cooperate."

He looked down at his watch.
"But just in case—prepare for Option Three."

CHAPTER 15
MEETING OF MINDS

6:47 PM – MinTech Private Offices, Perth

Christopher Fayes adjusted his cuffs, watching as Daniel and Clara entered the private conference room.

Daniel's jaw was tight. Clara looked calm but sharp, eyes scanning the room.

Smart.

He smiled, gesturing to the seats.

"Welcome. Please, sit."

They didn't move.

Daniel's voice was flat. "You've been chasing us across the state, and now you want to talk?"

Fayes gave an easy chuckle. "We could have done this the hard way. But I believe in options."

He slid a thin folder across the table.

Clara didn't take it. "What's this?"

"Your future," Fayes said smoothly.

Inside:
- A financial settlement—eight million dollars.
- A full NDA.
- A job offer for Daniel—editorial consulting, offshore.

A clean exit.

Daniel barely glanced at it. "You think this is about money?"

Fayes leaned forward, unruffled. "I think you're smart enough to take the easy way out."

Clara tilted her head. "And if we don't?"

Fayes exhaled, pretending to consider.

"Then you'll find that nobody believes ex-journalists and disgraced researchers."

He slid another file across the table.

Inside:
- False records linking Daniel to espionage.
- A fabricated history tying Clara to fraudulent research claims.
- A leak to the press is scheduled for 48 hours from now.

Daniel stiffened. Clara exhaled through her nose.

"This is what you do?" she said. "Silence people?"

Fayes smiled. "No, Miss Hayes. **We win.**"

Then, Fayes checked his watch and folded his hands neatly on the table.

"You have 24 hours to decide."

His eyes flicked between them, unreadable. "Take the deal, or lose everything."

He stood, smoothing his jacket. "I'll be expecting your call."

He gestured toward the door. Two security guards in suits stepped forward.

Clara didn't move.

She let the silence stretch, watching Hayes as he turned toward the exit.

Then—she spoke.

"What's with the boat in the desert?"

Fayes hesitated.

It was brief—half a second, maybe less—but Clara saw it.

A flicker.

Like a memory he'd been trained to forget.

Then, his expression smoothed back into cold indifference.

He turned his head slightly, lips curling into a smirk.

"Some questions aren't meant to be answered, Miss Hayes."

And with that, he walked out, leaving the folder sitting between them.

A final warning.

A final lie.

But now Clara knew one thing for certain.

The Kookaburra wasn't just a wreck.

It was a secret they were never supposed to find.

Daniel and Clara didn't resist as they were escorted toward the elevator.

The message was clear—MinTech wasn't throwing them out. They were keeping tabs on them.

They stepped inside, and Daniel pressed the button for the ground floor.

The doors slid shut.

Clara moved fast. She hit the button for the tenth floor, her breath catching as she waited.

For a moment, nothing happened.

Then—the lift slowed, coming to a halt.

She grabbed Daniel's sleeve. "Move."

The doors opened, and she pulled him into the corridor.

No alarms. No security.

Not yet.

She led him straight to the one place she knew there were no cameras.

The women's bathroom.

"We need proof," Clara whispered. "And I think I know where to find it."

Daniel frowned. "Where?"

A slow smile spread across her face. "The Manager's office."

Daniel groaned. "Oh, this is a terrible idea."

Clara ignored him. "Follow my lead."

They moved swiftly down the deserted corridor, footsteps muffled by the plush carpet. The office was dark, save for the glow of emergency exit signs and the faint hum of machines left on standby.

Rows of desks, filing cabinets, and a sleek, glass-walled manager's office sat at the end of the room.

Daniel exhaled sharply. "Tell me you know what you're doing."

Clara smirked. "Nope."

She crouched by the door, testing the handle. Locked.

Of course.

From her pocket, she pulled out a thin metal tool—not quite a lock pick, but close enough.

"Where the hell did you learn that?" Daniel whispered.

Clara didn't look up. "A misspent youth. Don't ask."

A soft click.

The door swung open.

They slipped inside, Daniel closing and locking the door behind them.

Searching for the Password

Clara moved fast, scanning the executive's desk.

No sticky notes. No scribbled passwords on notepads.

But she knew corporate types.

They never trusted IT.

They always kept backups somewhere.

Daniel rifled through the drawers, flipping through contracts, old memos, and useless paperwork.

Clara moved to the bookshelf, scanning the rows of binders and reference books.

Then—something stood out.

A leather-bound planner shoved beneath a stack of documents.

She pulled it free, flipping it open.

Meetings. Shipments. Operations schedules—and then, a single handwritten note buried in the margins.

"DATA: CONFIDENTIAL" – PW: M1N3X*2021

She held her breath.

"Got it."

Daniel arched a brow. "That's the password?"

Clara nodded, already moving toward the manager's computer.

Daniel stood near the door, keeping watch.

"You've got two minutes. Make it count."

The monitor flickered to life, the login screen prompting her for credentials.

Clara typed in the password, fingers flying across the keyboard.

For a second, nothing happened.

Then—the system unlocked.

She was in.

Files, emails, databases—MinTech's entire internal network at her fingertips.

Daniel moved closer. "What are you looking for?"

Clara navigated the server, searching through restricted directories.

Hidden files.

Then—she found it.

A folder labeled "QINGDAO EXPORT AGREEMENT".

Clara clicked it open.

Inside:

- Financial records linking MinTech to secret thorium shipments.
- Emails detailing how THO_2 was disguised as high-grade iron ore.
- A contract—MinTech's long-term deal with its Chinese buyers.

Clara air-dropped the files to her phone, the progress bar creeping forward.

She needed a backup.

Her fingers flew over the keyboard as she quickly drafted an email to Daniel's boss, attaching the files.

It was a long shot. MinTech's firewalls might block it, but at least it would create a digital trail—and while they were busy tracking the email, they wouldn't be looking for her phone.

She hit send.

Then—

A sharp footstep in the hallway.

Daniel stiffened. Not distant. Close.

They weren't alone.

CHAPTER 16
THE LAND REMEMBERS

The story was out.

Two days after Clara and Daniel vanished from MinTech's offices, an anonymous leak reached journalists across the country and eventually across the globe.

The headlines spread like wildfire.

- SECRET NUCLEAR EXPERIMENTS IN WESTERN AUSTRALIA
- MINTECH'S BILLION-DOLLAR COVER-UP
- A PROSPECTOR WHO DIED KNOWING TOO MUCH

MinTech denied everything.

The Australian government refused to comment.

But Clara knew better.

She sat in a quiet café in Scarborough, stirring her coffee as news anchors dissected the scandal. Footage of Port Hedland's shipments, blacked-out government records, and whispers of foreign involvement flooded the airwaves.

It was over.

Or at least—it should have been.

But something didn't sit right.

Daniel sat across from her, eyes flicking between the television and his laptop. His fingers hovered over the keys.

"What?" Clara asked.

Daniel didn't answer immediately. He turned the laptop to face her.

A document—one they hadn't sent to the press.

Jim Sullivan's final notes.

Clara's stomach clenched. "That wasn't in the leak."

Daniel exhaled. "I know. But someone uploaded it anyway."

The words stared back at her, scrawled in Jim's shaky handwriting.

They took it.

It wasn't gold.

I was never alone.

The land remembers.

A chill settled over her.

She had always thought of those words as a warning about MinTech. About the corporate greed, the buried history, the murders.

But what if Jim hadn't been talking about MinTech at all?
Her phone vibrated.
No name. No number.
Just three words.
"You dug too deep."
Clara's breath caught.
Her fingers tightened around the cup, knuckles white.
Daniel noticed. "What is it?"
She swallowed hard. "We missed something."
Outside, the city hummed with life—cars, pedestrians, the everyday chaos of Perth.
But for the first time since this started, Clara felt like she was being watched.
Her gaze drifted to the distant skyline—to the edge of the land where red dust met the ocean.
A memory flickered.
Clara didn't answer immediately. Her fingers tightened around her cup, knuckles white.
Outside, the city hummed with life—cars rushing past, neon reflections flickering across rain-slick pavement.
But for the first time since this started, she felt it.
She was being watched.
The sensation crept up her spine, cold and certain, like standing too close to the edge of a drop-off. She forced herself to turn, scanning the café's interior.
Nothing.
But that feeling remained.
Her gaze drifted past the windows—to the distant skyline, to the edge of the land where red dust met the ocean.
Something about that horizon felt wrong.
Like a whisper she couldn't quite hear.
A memory flickered—something buried, something she hadn't pieced together.
Jim Sullivan.
His name had been everywhere in the MinTech files.
But there was something off about the way he vanished.
Something more than just a prospector who saw too much.
Clara exhaled sharply.
"I need to know more about Jim."
Daniel blinked. "Why?"
She hesitated, then set down her cup. "Because I think we missed something. And I think someone wants to make sure we never find it."

Digging into Jim's Past, Clara dug through online archives.
Old newspaper scans, half-remembered stories from the gold rush days, the same blurred photo of Jim Sullivan standing outside a Kalgoorlie pub.

None of it told her what she needed to know.

Clara pushed further. Police records.

And then—she found it.

A report.

Dated 1911.

Subject: Incident Report – Half Moon Watering Hole

Filed By: Constable Edwin Cooper

Details: Mr. Sullivan turned over a quantity of gold to authorities. Claimed to have found it near Half Moon Watering Hole. Witnesses reported he was rambling about a man named Paddy O'Rourke.

Clara froze.

Jim Sullivan.

His name was everywhere in the MinTech files, but this was different. This wasn't about thorium or secret mining operations.

This was personal.

Her fingers flew over the keyboard as she dug deeper—old police logs, newspaper clippings, archived immigration records.

A single name surfaced again and again.

Paddy O'Rourke.

Buried. Forgotten. Lost in the archives.

Until now.

Her breath caught as she read the next entry.

Name: Patrick "Paddy" O'Rourke

Date of Birth: 1874

Gold Miner, Western Australia

Last Known Location: Half Moon Watering Hole, 1911

Presumed Dead. No remains recovered.

She stared at the words.

Presumed dead.

But not confirmed.

Her eyes narrowed. There was more.

Another document surfaced—decades later.

A different Paddy O'Rourke.

Born: 1912.

Son of a man with no listed birth certificate. No parents. No past.

A man who had arrived in Western Australia with nothing—except a name.

Clara's stomach twisted.

Paddy O'Rourke hadn't vanished.

He had walked away.

And his descendants…?

Her pulse pounded as she flipped through another document.

A family record.

She turned to Daniel, the weight of her discovery sinking in.

Daniel frowned. "What?"

Clara exhaled. "It's you."

Daniel blinked. "What the hell are you talking about?"

She turned the laptop screen towards Daniel.

The final statement from Jim Sullivan before his release: "He didn't run. He didn't fall. He was taken."

Daniel's fingers tightened around the paper. "You're saying…"

Clara nodded.

"Paddy O'Rourke never disappeared."

"He started over."

Daniel's chest rose and fell, slow and measured.

"Are you telling me…" He swallowed. "This whole time—"

"This whole time," Clara whispered, "you've been chasing your own damn family."

Silence stretched between them.

Daniel let out a shaky breath. "Wow."

Was Daniel, Paddy O'Rourke's blood?

And he had never known.

Final statement before release:

"He didn't run. He didn't fall. He was taken."Daniel frowned. "Okay… but —"

Clara slid another document across the table.

A family record.

Paddy O'Rourke had **not disappeared.** He had started a new life. And his descendants?

Daniel's family.

Daniel swallowed hard. "You're telling me I've been chasing this story, and the whole time—it's been about my own damn family?"

Clara nodded. "Not a coincidence, Daniel."

She read the last line again and again.

Daniel leaned over her shoulder. "What the hell does that mean?"

She swallowed. "It means… Jim was scared."

Daniel exhaled. "Clara, he was a prospector in 1911. People vanished all the time. Got lost. Fell into sinkholes. Got killed for their gold."

Clara shook her head.

"No. That's not what this is."

She tapped the police report. "Look at what he said."

Shadows moving.

The land remembers.

"He was taken."

She looked at Daniel, her pulse quickening.

"This wasn't about MinTech. Not then."

Daniel ran a hand through his hair. "You think he was talking about the Wunambi."

Clara nodded.

Daniel sighed. "Okay. So let's say the stories have some truth. What do you expect to find over a hundred years later?"

Clara exhaled, staring at the report.

"I don't know. But I need to see where it happened."

CHAPTER 17
THE WUNAMBI'S WARNINGS

She had spent so much time looking at MinTech, but Jim's final words weren't just about what humans had done.
They were about what was already there.
The land remembers.
And so did they.
The café's television flickered.
Static, for a brief second.
Then—the power cut out.
Daniel sat up straighter. "What the hell?"
Clara's phone screen went black.
No warning. No reboot.
Just—darkness.
A slow, uneasy sensation crept over her skin.
Daniel met her gaze. "Tell me I'm not crazy."
Clara exhaled. "I don't think we were the only ones watching."
The story was out.
But the real truth was still buried.
And whatever Jim Sullivan had found all those years ago—
It wasn't finished with them yet.
The story had gone global.
MinTech's cover-up was public, their shipments halted, and their executives under investigation. Daniel's exposé had made international headlines.
But Clara couldn't shake the feeling that something was still missing.
A warning she had ignored.
Jim's words—"The land remembers."
The message—"You dug too deep."
And then, the one question that had never been answered:
Why was there a wooden boat in the desert?

Clara sat alone in the dim motel room, the glow of her laptop illuminating faded police records.
Jim Sullivan's original interview—the one from when he had handed over the gold.
She skimmed the transcript, her heart beginning to pound.
Q: Where did you find it?
JIM SULLIVAN: Half Moon Watering Hole.

Q: And you said someone else was with you?
JIM SULLIVAN: Paddy O'Rourke. He was the one who saw it first.
Q: And where is Mr. O'Rourke now?
JIM SULLIVAN: I don't know. He disappeared that night. Just… gone.

Clara froze.

She cross-referenced the name.

Paddy O'Rourke.

The records were sparse. Born in the late 1800s. Came to Australia during the gold rush. Irish descent. Vanished without a trace.

She kept digging. Ancestry records. Old census documents.

And then—Daniel's family tree.

Her breath caught.

Daniel O'Rourke. Descendant of Patrick O'Rourke.

She stared at the screen.

This wasn't a coincidence.

Daniel had always been part of this.

He just never knew.

It stretched all the way back—to Half Moon Watering Hole, 1896.

She didn't tell him everything right away.

Not until they stood at the edge of Half Moon Watering Hole, the same place Jim and Paddy had made their fateful discovery.

The desert stretched endless before them, the heat pressing down like a silent weight.

Daniel adjusted his pack, squinting at the horizon. "So, what exactly are we hoping to find?"

Clara reached into her bag, pulling out the gifts they had brought.

A peace offering.

- Ochre, gathered from the land itself.
- A smudge stick of eucalyptus leaves, bound tightly.
- A small carved wooden snake figurine—Wunambi's likeness, a sign of respect.
- And finally, a long polished stone blade—shaped by a father's father, carrying the weight of the land's old power.

Daniel frowned. "You think this will… calm the Wunambi?"

Clara hesitated.

It wasn't just a hope. It was a warning—one that had been given long ago.

She thought of Jim Sullivan's journal, of the faded ink scrawled in his frantic hand. The old man's words, recorded in half-legible script:

"Light the leaves with fire. Breathe the smoke. It will cleanse the bad spirits from you. And the carving of Wunambi will show him you mean respect."

Clara's grip tightened around the blade.

She turned to Daniel, voice low. "I don't think. I know."

Clara's voice was steady. "I think the land has been waiting."

She stepped forward, placing the offerings gently at the base of a rock at the edge of Half Moon watering hole.

The wind shifted.
A stillness settled over the area, the air thick with something unseen.
Daniel swallowed. "Alright. Now what?"
Clara looked out at the desert.
"Now we listen."

The Land Remembers

The first sound was a whisper.
Not the wind. Not the shifting sands.
Something older.
Daniel felt it too—a hum beneath his feet, a vibration deep in his bones.
Clara's breath caught in her throat. "Daniel—look."
The water ahead of them—shifted.
Not a mirage. Not the heat.
The land itself was moving.
Daniel stepped back, instinct screaming at him. But Clara didn't run.
She knelt, fingers brushing the earth, skimming the surface of the water.
The ground was warm.
And then—the shadows stretched.
A figure.
Tall. Elongated. Not human.
Daniel's pulse pounded. He knew this shape.
The Wunambi.
Jim had seen them.
Paddy had seen them.
And now—so had they.
The air grew heavy, electric.
Clara placed her hand over the ochre, pressing it into the dirt.
A whisper drifted through the air, words neither of them spoke.
But Daniel understood.
This was not a warning.
It was a reminder.
The land had always remembered.
Now—it was up to them to do the same.

The MinTech story had shaken the world.
But what Clara and Daniel had discovered?
That was never meant to be known.
Their article was published in fragments—not the full truth, just enough.
Because some things weren't meant to be written.
Some truths belonged only to the land.
And some names—Paddy O'Rourke. Jim Sullivan. The ones who had come before—
Would never be forgotten.
As the world chased its corporate scandals and buried nuclear experiments, Clara and Daniel stood at the edge of something much older.

Something watching.
Something waiting.
And for the first time since this all began—
Clara knew how the story really ended.
The land remembers.
And now, so did they.

EPILOGUE

March 15, 2025

The arid expanse of the Australian Outback stretched endlessly under the scorching sun, a land that had long guarded its secrets beneath layers of red earth and time. Yet, recent discoveries had begun to unravel one of its most enigmatic mysteries: the presence of a wooden boat, weathered by age, found nestled deep within the desert sands.

Beneath Australia's parched surface lies the Great Artesian Basin (GAB), one of the largest underground freshwater reservoirs globally, spanning approximately 22% of the continent. This vast aquifer system has, over millennia, carved out intricate networks of subterranean channels and caverns, some stretching for hundreds of kilometres. These hidden waterways have been the lifeblood for many ecosystems and indigenous communities, providing sustenance in an otherwise unforgiving landscape.

The discovery of the boat, now identified as The Kookaburra, has been linked to these ancient underground watercourses. Researchers hypothesise that during periods of significant rainfall or climatic shifts, these subterranean channels could have become navigable, allowing vessels like The Kookaburra to traverse regions that are now arid deserts. Over time, as water levels receded and courses shifted, the boat became stranded, buried by the encroaching sands.

Compounding the mystery, traces of thorium—a mildly radioactive element—were discovered within the boat's cargo hold. Thorium has been recognised for its potential in nuclear energy generation, particularly within the thorium fuel cycle, which offers a safer and more abundant alternative to traditional uranium-based reactors. An article published on August 2, 2013, in Australian Mining delved into the energy potential of thorium, highlighting its advantages, including reduced long-lived radioactive waste and enhanced safety features.

The presence of thorium in The Kookaburra suggests that the vessel might have been part of early experimental endeavours to explore alternative energy sources. Given the clandestine nature of such projects during that era, it's plausible that these experiments were conducted away from populated areas, deep within Australia's interior. The boat's journey through the subterranean waterways could have been an attempt to transport thorium discreetly, ensuring that any potential risks remained isolated.

In light of these revelations, MinTech, a leading entity in the mining and energy sector, has acknowledged the profound significance of these findings, both scientifically and culturally. Recognising the enduring connection between the Indigenous communities and the land—communities that have relied on the Great Artesian Basin's resources for thousands of years—MinTech has established the Wunambi Foundation.

Named to honour the Indigenous lore of the Wunambi, a mythical serpent believed to inhabit the subterranean waterways, the foundation aims to:

- Cultural Preservation: Document and safeguard Indigenous stories, traditions, and knowledge related to the land and its hidden watercourses.

- Sustainable Resource Management: Collaborate with Indigenous leaders to develop practices that ensure the responsible use of the Great Artesian Basin's resources, balancing ecological health with community needs.

- Educational Initiatives: Provide scholarships and funding for Indigenous youth to pursue studies in environmental science, geology, and cultural studies, fostering a new generation of custodians for their ancestral lands.

MinTech's CEO, Ella Shadow, emphasised the company's dedication to reconciliation and mutual growth: "We are not just uncovering geological and historical artefacts; we are reconnecting with the narratives of the land's first inhabitants. Through the Wunambi Foundation, we aspire to build a future where technological advancement and traditional wisdom walk hand in hand."

As the sun set over the Outback, casting long shadows over the red dirt, Clara stood at the edge of the excavation site. The air was thick with the scent of eucalyptus, and the distant call of a kookaburra echoed—a haunting reminder of the land's timelessness.

Holding the polished stone blade gifted by the elders, she felt the weight of history and responsibility. The journey to uncover The Kookaburra's secrets had been arduous, filled with more questions than answers. Yet, amidst the uncertainties, one truth remained clear: the land, with its hidden waterways and ancient tales, held stories waiting to be told.

With renewed determination, Clara pledged to continue her quest—not just for accolades but to honour the legacy of those who had come before and to ensure that the lessons of the past would guide the future.

And so, under the vast Australian sky, the narrative of The Kookaburra, the subterranean rivers, and the intertwined destinies of a land and its people flowed on, like the hidden waters beneath the desert, carving their path through time.

While the world focused on The Kookaburra and the implications of thorium in Australia's energy landscape, Daniel O'Rourke found himself consumed by a different kind of mystery—his own family history.

With every new document unearthed, the truth became harder to ignore. He had spent his entire career chasing stories, never realising he was part of one.

Daniel sat at his desk, scanning over immigration records, marriage certificates, and faded police reports. Patrick 'Paddy' O'Rourke. His great-great great grandfather. The man who had supposedly vanished at Half Moon Watering Hole in 1911. Presumed dead. But not confirmed.

If the records were accurate, Paddy had not disappeared—he had left the goldfields behind, taking on a new journey, cutting ties with his past. The O'Rourke line had continued, unknowingly passing down a history that had been erased from official records.

His fingers traced over a grainy, black-and-white photograph from 1908. A man standing beside Jim Sullivan. A man who bore an uncanny resemblance to his own father.

"This whole time…" Daniel exhaled. "I was looking for a story, and I was the story."

Clara had been right. There were no coincidences.

Days later, Daniel and Clara returned to Half Moon Watering Hole. Not as journalists but as seekers of truth.

They stood at the water's edge, the ochre-stained cliffs towering around them. The land was silent as if waiting.

Daniel reached into his bag, pulling out a small, carved wooden serpent similar to the gift the elders had once given Paddy O'Rourke, now placed back where it belonged.

"We come with respect," Clara murmured.
The wind shifted. The still surface of the water rippled.
Then—
A sound cut through the air. A deep, resonant scream.

Not human. Not of this world.

Daniel's breath caught, every instinct screamed at him to run, but he stood his ground. He had spent his life dismissing legends, reducing them to stories and superstition. But standing here now, he knew better.

The land remembered. And the Wunambi had never left.

ABOUT THE AUTHOR

Having lived in five countries and embraced three different citizenships, I have spent my life searching for a place to belong. Now settled in Western Australia, I continue to navigate the complexities of identity, culture, and the ever-present contrast between my personal values and the traditions of the country I was born into. This journey has often left me feeling like an outsider —neither fully accepted nor truly at home—but it has also driven my deep curiosity and commitment to understanding the cultures around me.

Through books and studies, I have always sought to learn from the history, languages, and ideologies of the places I've called home. As part of this journey, I have studied the basic Noongar language and engaged with the stories of First Nations peoples. This work is a fictional narrative, inspired by a small fraction of places and people I've met, written with the deepest respect. My aim is not to offend but to open a door—to encourage understanding, conversation, and greater inclusion between the people.

AUTHOR'S NOTE

This story is inspired by the rich tapestry of Western Australia's Goldfields during the 1896 Kalgoorlie Gold Rush—a time of hardship, hope, and human ambition. The world of tent cities, water scarcity, and feverish prospecting draws from historical accounts and the spirit captured in works like The Goldrush Era by Geoffrey Blainey, as well as newspapers of the time, including The Kalgoorlie Miner. While this narrative is fictional, it pays homage to the true grit of those who ventured into the red dust in search of fortune.

The inclusion of Wongi (Wangkatha) culture, including the mythic Wunambi, is a respectful fictional interpretation of Aboriginal spirituality. I acknowledge the Wongi people, traditional custodians of the Kalgoorlie region, and pay my respects to Elders past and present. Elements of Dreamtime lore have been drawn from general public knowledge, with the intent to honour, not appropriate. Any errors are my own.

Inspiration also came from Australia's geological mysteries—like the presence of ancient marine fossils in the desert—and tales of oddities like stranded ships in unlikely places. The Kookaburra and its peculiar cargo, while fictional, echo real-world maritime legends and geological anomalies. Masonic elements in the story nod to the historical presence of Freemasonry in early Australian mining communities, where such symbols often carried power and secrecy.

This work emerged from a deep fascination with the collision of cultures, lost histories, and the surreal truths often hidden beneath the sand. No specific sources were harmed in the making—just fueled by imagination, curiosity, and a love of strange tales.

Made in the USA
Columbia, SC
11 April 2025